MY LIFE AS AN ANIMAL

MY LIFE AS AN ANIMAL

STORIES

LAURIE STONE

TriQuarterly Books
Northwestern University Press
Evanston, Illinois

TriQuarterly Books
Northwestern University Press
www.nupress.northwestern.edu

Copyright © 2017 by Laurie Stone. Published 2017 by TriQuarterly Books /
Northwestern University Press. All rights reserved.

Printed in the United States of America

10 9 8 7 6 5 4 3 2 1

Library of Congress Cataloging-in-Publication Data
Names: Stone, Laurie (Novelist), author.
Title: My life as an animal : stories / Laurie Stone.
Description: Evanston, Illinois : TriQuarterly Books / Northwestern University
    Press, 2017.
Identifiers: LCCN 2016013829 | ISBN 9780810134287 (pbk. : alk. paper) |
    ISBN 9780810134294 (e-book)
Classification: LCC PS3569.T64137 A6 2016 | DDC 813.54—dc23
LC record available at http://lccn.loc.gov/2016013829

for Richard

CONTENTS

MY LIFE AS AN ANIMAL

YARD SALE

For a while Richard and I lived in a small condo apartment in Scottsdale, unsure if we were staying in Arizona. Ikea furniture fit. Lobby furniture: stylish and impersonal. Among the pieces we bought was a glass-topped table on a metal scaffold, meant for dining. When it turned out we didn't like sitting down to meals, I commandeered it for my desk.

I see an identical table on Craigslist. Ikea no longer sells them, and now that Richard has landed his dream job, teaching at the university, I have formed an image of us at separate glass tables, like dueling pianists, but on opposite sides of the big house we have rented. On the phone the seller sounds blurry, but he lives nearby and is willing to deliver. His name is Jeff. Richard and I drive to Jeff's careworn street and pull up to a dusty yard dotted with cacti left stunned in death poses. Jeff is outside, a tall, burly man, and the table is beside him, coated with dust. I don't inspect it carefully before offering him seventy-five dollars. He says, "Okay." Afterward, Richard will say, "You could have gotten it for less," and I think he is right and feel a little bad, but I let it go because I was in the moment with Jeff, whose face looks like beef jerky.

The table has not seen the inside of the house. Maybe Jeff won it in a poker game the night before. He pockets the cash and goes to work wrapping the table in blankets and gently positioning it in the center of his pickup. Later, Richard will say, "He was high as a kite, didn't you notice?" I will say, "No." I don't see what Richard sees. It is one of the reasons I like floating along beside him. He teaches museum studies, and being with him is like being with a tour guide, and it makes me feel we are permanent tourists, even in the place where we live.

Jeff has chairs to sell, and we enter his house. A plastic curtain separates the front from the back, and the floors are dirt. There is no floor. It's like a construction site, with beer cans and pizza boxes strewn around. I don't see any furniture. The scene is desperate, but I am attracted to the whittled-down look. At yard sales, I feel an impulse to dive into other people's stuff and then go home and sell everything we have.

Jeff slips into a back room and returns with a rattan chair. It is not our thing, and we pass outside. The air is filmy and pink. Distant outcroppings cast jagged shadows on mountains that ring the valley. Richard climbs into Jeff's truck, and I drive my car. Back at our place, Jeff settles the table in our garage and lingers a little before taking off. After he leaves, Richard says, "He talked the whole time about missing his wife. She left him. He told me about a hunting trip he went on with his son. It was sad." Richard sighs, looking for a bush to dump Jeff's troubles on, and we are reminded of the difference between shopping at a yard sale and buying something in a store. In a store, you imagine you are witnessing the birth of an object. At yard sales, you carry away a little of the person, and they are left with your expression as you gazed with admiration at something that was theirs.

What am I looking for? Why can some people attach themselves to houses, communities, families? Or is that a myth? Does everyone enter such entanglements with secret dread?

If Richard and I were in Paris, we would repair to our favorite grand café, sipping *café crème* and catching the passing chic. We would live in a country where philosophers are rock stars. If we were in Berlin, we would haunt a graffitied outpost of punk and watch redheaded blade runners race for trams. We would smell history in shards of the wall, see imprints of tanks, picture machine guns and hoods of terror. If we were in London, we would visit our neighborhood pub and contemplate the multi-culti collage. If we were in New York, we would know every gallery, bar, and vest pocket patch of green. We would cross the Brooklyn Bridge, peering down at the river with its artist-made waterfalls. We would slither through Chinatown, lurk in DUMBO shadows, discover streets where we were strangers.

People say, "You have to find something to love besides Richard in the place where you have come. You have to find the desert in you." My friend Angeles says, "People are more creative in exile from their physical home. You discover unknown places in yourself."

Before Richard and I moved out of the condo apartment, we threw a yard sale of our own, and as Richard was rummaging in the garage, he found the garment bag I had carried to Arizona from New York. It was an expensive LeSportsac, and now it was a crumpled black thing you couldn't identify, and Richard was crinkling his nose and saying, "It smells like old cheese." The bag was stinking from the heat and couldn't be used anymore. I threw it in the trash, remembering the spring of 2007, the way I had walked from the plane and spotted Richard at the end of the ramp, looking like an arrow with his slim body and silver hair, and the hard little spike that holds me up just melted.

Next to the garment bag was a box Richard had packed when he left his wife. Inside the box were snapshots from the 1980s, when he lived in Leeds with a woman named Kim. In the photographs he is thirty, and he stares out, unsmiling. His hair is brown and thick, and it flops over his forehead, and he wears large glasses and seems wary. He looks like someone an anthropologist would discover behind a tree. That is how Richard always looks in photographs, like he's been seized by authorities and is awaiting deportation back to England.

As we were setting up our sale, a large woman got out of her car and began looking at our stuff. Her hair was blond and thinning, and she wore it pulled back in a clasp. I could see her scalp glistening with sweat as she stood in the sun, and my heart went out to her, and I wondered if my hair looked thin. I wondered if I was too old to attract someone other than Richard. It was early in the morning but already the kind of hot that rubs you like a rusty gate. The woman asked if we had jewelry, and I showed her a silver pin in the shape of a fleur-de-lis Richard had squirreled away in a drawer. She held it up and said, "How much?" I said, "Two dollars." She said, "I'll take it." We exchanged smiles.

She fanned her face, saying she was caring for her mother, who was sick and had come to live with her. She was looking for conversation. It was the reason I went anywhere, and I remembered my mother when we lived in Washington Heights in the 1950s, the way she would dress to leave the apartment, a girdle and makeup to meet strangers. Not exactly strangers. The butcher, let's say. She would wait for her turn to face him across the counter, a man with a bloody apron stretched tight across his paunch, and they would consult about brisket, Jew to Jew in the sawdust, and you could sense the despair of the carcasses hanging in the back, and it would make the occasion tender, all of us feeling closer to the chopping block. After my mother left the butcher's, she would visit the dry cleaner's and the post office, and St. Nicholas Avenue would vibrate to the rhythm of her high heels clip-clopping on the pavement.

The blond woman said her mother had emphysema. On weekends, to give herself a break, she drove to yard sales. The more she talked, the more she gathered, including a beaded belt buckle and a leather bomber jacket with a mouton lining. When would she wear a coat like this in Arizona? A place where temperatures soar past one hundred and twenty degrees in summer and baby desert squirrels cook in their holes or dry to crisps along trails. Maybe the coat would remind her of our meeting.

I told her my mother had had a stroke some years earlier and for a long time my sister and I had circled her in a tight little orbit. It was a period when I wanted to live anywhere but New York, and then I met Richard and felt I had nothing to lose. Really, I had nothing to lose. After Richard left his wife, he rented a tiny flat with two red leather couches and two enormous TVs. We would stretch out on the couches, listening to Bob Dylan and Leonard Cohen, who sounded like Jewish uncles, dispensing advice on love and sex. When I hooked up with Richard, I did not think about my mother's exit from Manhattan in the 1950s, when we moved to Long Beach full-time. Parted from her streets and plunked into a world of mahjong games and beach clubs, she looked like she had fallen under a spell.

My mother said she did not like games, but there she was at the Malibu Beach Club, shifting mahjong tiles that made a clicking sound like hard candy hitting your teeth. Before I moved to Arizona, she said, "Don't go," and I thought she was saying, "You can't have love." I thought she was saying, "The love you have found is empty as a desert." As she neared death, she would ask, "What's it all about?" And I would wonder how, if you hated games, you could master something as intricate as mahjong, and I would think, If you could accomplish something like that, what else might you have made of your life?

At yard sales, I am in training for something, although there is no contest at the end. There is no end, and maybe that is the attraction. Some people hold garage sales every weekend, as if they were running a shop. You can tell from the prices and their boredom. There is no story. The other day I wandered through the house of a dead woman, inspecting her menorahs and Sabbath plates, cruising past her hair brushes, tangled with gray strands, and her leather shoes etched with her bunions. No one wanted these things. The scene was creepy yet intimate. Something familiar. Something familiar you have never seen before.

I was sighing as I pulled up to yet another yard scattered with baby clothes, snarled Christmas lights, and half-empty jugs of automotive fluids. People like to sit out on lawn chairs—but really. I was asking myself, What are you doing? Then I rounded a corner and saw a driveway heaped with elegant furniture and boxes of luxurious pottery and linens. The neighborhood was not chic. You just never know. People were swarming over a life coming apart or being set free. Three men aged around thirty-five or forty were negotiating deals, and suddenly, maybe for the first time in Arizona, I knew where I was. I was in a club on the Lower East Side with gay boys. They seemed gay, but it was partly their deadpan

My Life as an Animal

delivery, tossing the buyers a quick once-over to decide what they would charge, lowering the price if they liked you.

At the center was Shane. People were calling out his name. He was wearing a blue suit jacket and looked puffy from late nights out. I went up to him and said, "Shane, what are you doing, what is going on here?" He said, "I don't know, but all this has to go," and he winced as people handled his possessions, not roughly but with the dispassion of hawks circling a rabbit. I did not feel like robbing him. Well, I did, but there was conflict. The other day I was struggling to find a phrase I could taste but could not coax into my brain mouth. I thought the phrase was at the core of who I was and therefore the reason it was hiding. I worked on something else for a while, and then the phrase floated up, *to have designs on*, and I understood why I love yard sales, where you are free to pounce openly on other people's stuff.

In one of Shane's boxes nestled large, decorative bottles of peppers and olives, the kind you see in Little Italy, and I asked if he was in the restaurant business. He shook his head and said, "No, we just liked nice things." A truck arrived with more furniture, and Shane said things would be coming out of storage all day and tomorrow. His heart was broken. None of this mattered, and he flipped open his phone to show me pictures of a three-year-old girl beside a pretty woman with red hair. His daughter and wife were in California and would not be returning. He didn't explain. What was the story? Love dies? Businesses fail?

In Arizona, the economy is boom or bust, and we were in a bust phase, with real estate deals going south and the population in a rapid churn. In Scottsdale and neighboring parts of Phoenix, people who hold yard sales are generally weeding their belongings to make room for more. Others are relocating to California or Hawaii. The drift is invariably west, toward a place imagined as lush and golden, as if, like Willy Loman's brother Ben, people are lighting out for diamonds and adventure. In the mix of sellers are people who are downsizing, as they say, their faces strained by thoughts of their dicey mortgage deals. Sometimes, you see a look of hope and freedom, too—but only on the young. One day Richard and I met a kind-faced woman in her seventies who was on the brink of surrendering her house to the bank and moving to a studio flat. It was nearly Christmas, and she had been selling her things since Halloween. She was sad but showed no self-pity. Her plants were lined up along the driveway. She would have no place to keep them and she was giving them away. We bought two.

It was difficult for Shane to set prices on his belongings, so when a customer approached, I whispered a figure to him, and he repeated it to the person with a crooked smile. He wanted to recoup the worth of his things, but he could see it was impossible, and it seemed we were floating out together on a tide. I found an unopened box of cookies. Shane said, "You eat one first." I opened the box and popped a cookie in my mouth. It was made of maple syrup and butter. I said, "It's good. It tastes like a crepe." Shane broke off a piece and ate it. "It is good," he said. In time, I found a mahogany salad bowl, a set of bar tools, and a hinged box shaped like a small pumpkin. Shane practically gave them to me. I told him I had come to Arizona for love and that our house was pretty much empty. He said, "Come back tomorrow." He said, "Take my cell number, but don't call me at three in the morning." I said, "That is when I would most want to talk to you."

Richard asks what I learn about myself at yard sales. He says, "You are so focused on the hunt you don't see how you

My Life as an Animal

are perceived." How do we know how we are perceived? The day I met Shane, I was wearing wrinkled clothes, and my hair was a snaggle out of bed. Richard says he knows how he is perceived, and yet often after a party he will ask, "Did they think I was smart? Did they like me?"

The next day I returned to Shane's place, and when I got out of the car we held each other close. It was as if we were at an airport, meeting and separating at the same time. I bought a table for Richard's studio, and now, whenever I look at the green legs and butcher-block inlays, I wonder what Shane is doing and where he has gone. I think of calling him, although I have not. In Arizona, the people I know are Richard's friends. In New York, we see my friends. Most of the time in Arizona I am in the house, writing. To know people here you need a job. Some days driving to yard sales is my job.

On Monday I read an ad on Craigslist. A seller is joining the Marines and has to clear an apartment by Friday. I leave a message, and a woman calls back, explaining she is the one enlisting. Her name is Taylor, and her voice is hearty and sweet. She sounds like she could bench-press you over her head and settle you down gently again. She tells me to come to her condo the next day. Her boyfriend, Brandon, will be there to show me around, and, sure enough, as Richard and I pull up, a slight young man with a shy smile is waiting outside one of the cubes in a nondescript compound. Richard waits in the car, reading.

Brandon has a short cap of brown hair and dark, melting eyes. He is wearing loose-fitting clothes, and his feet are bare. He has a limp. I follow him up a flight of stairs and ask if he is joining up, too. He says, "No, I can't." I say, "Good," and he turns, and after a hesitation a light in his eyes switches on like one of those energy-conserving fluorescent bulbs.

He says he wishes he could enlist, but he's damaged. He uses the word *damaged*, not *injured*. The nerves in his hands and legs don't work properly, he says, and I can see he's a little jittery and unsteady, just the slightest bit. He says it's from mountain biking, all the times he's gone careening down and crashed hard on rocks. He's maybe twenty-one. He flashes a sad smile, explaining the Marines won't take him, but he is going off with Taylor, possibly to Okinawa, and I can see by the way he says her name, his face opening like a shade lifting on a window, he is madly in love with her.

Their small apartment is crammed with boxes and furniture. A plump, blond woman is on the couch, her back very straight as she speaks with an older man, and I can't tell if they know each other or have just met. I am not introduced. It's as if I am not there or the blond woman isn't visible or doesn't want to be. I overhear her tell the man that her husband was burned on a mission in Vietnam. She is Taylor's mother or Brandon's, maybe, and I realize I have entered a military family and should keep my mouth shut about enlisting.

I snoop around like a detective without a search warrant, thinking I should warn Brandon to hide the silver and lock up the chickens. I wish I could be a real wolf, who dines without conscience on those he has fooled, but I like Brandon. The kitchen is well stocked. It turns out Taylor is a chef and works at one of the restaurants in the pricey chain Ruth's Chris Steak House. I organize a pile of whisks, measuring cups, knives, and a Microplane. Brandon offers me a tin of Godiva chocolate, and I find a box of Swiffers and two houseplants. We settle on fifteen dollars for the lot, and as he helps me carry the things to the car, I ask if he regrets mountain biking. He shoots me a wide grin and says,

"No," emphatically, and I think about Richard's question, "What do you learn in these encounters?" and I think it is how easily I fall in love with strangers and what they are willing to reveal. Richard loads the car, and as Brandon and I say good-bye I kiss him lightly on the cheek, and he looks a little startled, but he stands outside waving until we are out of sight.

In my favorite yard sales, I feel I am entering a play. You don't know what has preceded your scene or what will follow it. With strangers, I feel I can say whatever floats into my head, and it reminds me of my mother, who preferred not to rein herself in and who was probably incapable of it. Richard and I are at Starbucks, and he says, "At a yard sale you have to know you want something, and what it might be worth, and what you are willing to offer. You have to know these things fast, and I find that confusing. I don't care enough." Actually, he is skillful at unearthing treasures. He discovered a wooden bowl we bought for fifty cents that proved to be hand turned, rare, and signed. He spotted a teak, Danish modern coffee table standing forlornly on a dusty driveway. We bought it for ten dollars. I did the deals. He sips his latte and says, "In the world I come from, paying retail shows you *can afford* to pay retail."

Richard's father was a bespoke tailor who fashioned hand-made clothes. There was a shop in their house, where customers came for fittings. But his father did not want to be a tailor, and the children were not allowed in the shop. The family were shopkeepers, and the family were not shopkeepers. Richard dislikes rooting around in other people's stuff because he thinks he is stirring up embarrassment.

The other morning we were in bed, and I was telling him about people I had lost by disregarding a boundary. Milky light was easing through the glass doors that look out to a desert garden and a sparkling swimming pool. I was remembering friends whose feelings I had hurt or whose generosity I had imposed on, and Richard slipped his arm around my shoulder and stroked me.

This summer, I will pack up my apartment in Manhattan, feeling like an interloper at a funeral. I will surrender a rent-stabilized apartment on the Upper West Side. If I had a religion, this would be its only sacrilege. I will open closets and wonder, Who wore these boots? My feet are no longer the feet of those shoes. I will pack Gardner's paintings and furniture. Gardner, a man I loved, has been dead for twenty years. Once you change the setting of an object, what does it become? Bones in the ground are different from bones on your plate or bones inside a glass case. The leash of my dog will hang on the doorknob. I will pack it. I will not pack it. Sasha has been dead nearly as long as Gardner. Richard and I will rent a truck and drive to a desert that holds no meaning for either of us.

Often, it seems, building up and tearing down are simultaneous activities. I visit my friend Carrie, who says, "Help me." I say, "Okay." She says, "You won't want to do this." I say, "What?" She says, "Sell Belle's stuff." We are on the screened porch of her house in Hudson, New York. The roof is high, and you don't feel penned in, and there are tall, green trees everywhere: oaks, maples, birches. I am in love with the greenness and bendy deciduousness of these trees, even though, before living in Arizona, I did not notice them much.

Carrie and I are at a picnic table. The bench cushions are covered in colorful fabric from Guatemala, Bali, and Bangladesh, places Carrie and Belle traveled to. They were married, and Belle has been dead for a year. Belle was a

My Life as an Animal

collector, and I appreciate the spill of her stuff. You walk into a bathroom, and the shelves sag with lotions and gels. Carrie is depressed. There is too much Belle around for her not to sink. She says, "I wish I liked to drink because I could start at noon and be unconscious all day. You can't take Ambien at noon." I say, "Why not?" She smiles.

She lays out Belle's clothes on a bed: silk pajamas, tunics, smoking jackets. Faded pinks with satin ribbons at the necks. A long, cream-colored smock Isadora Duncan might have worn flitting through the bendy trees. Carrie asks if I want anything, turning away.

A couple of weeks ago, I met a couple on Craigslist who were downsizing, a man and a woman in matching training suits. The furniture they were selling had belonged to the man's parents. I bought a blond console table with tapered legs and a tall metal floor lamp with three halogen lights that swivel in different directions. I paid forty-five dollars for both, and the couple were pleased, but as the man helped me load my car, a wistful look crossed his eyes that surprised him. I was carting away his childhood, and we all felt the tug.

At another sale, a woman was emptying a house because her mother was too old and infirm to live there anymore. I found a panel of leaded glass in an oak frame—a vivid, art nouveau motif of flowers against a smoky green background. At home, Richard rested the panel against a small, white cube lamp, and the room shimmered into life. The effect was astonishing. At the sale, the woman, near tears, said, "My mother made that." She wanted me to know its value, and I said I would take care of it. When my mother died, I had two weeks to clear her apartment, and I was in a rage about her death or her life. I jettisoned her belongings as if I could rid myself of her. I wish I had not.

Gently, I say to Carrie, "I don't need anything." She says, "Okay" and leaves the room and returns with a box of silver earrings tarnished black. She doesn't want to polish them. She says, "Help me find a place for them. Help me take them to a consignment shop." I say, "What a good idea," hoping we will sell all of Belle's belongings on the spot.

Carrie says, "After a year, I thought it would get better, but when I came back from Japan . . ." She pauses, and I think she is going to say, "I expected to see Belle on the couch." She doesn't finish the thought. She sinks onto the bed and says she is eating ice cream for all of her meals. She says, "I eat a pint of coffee Häagen-Dazs for the main course and a pint of strawberry for dessert." She says she is fat, pinching her sides. I see she is heavier, and that she has let her hair go gray. I don't care. We have been friends for forty-five years. I made friends before I went to kindergarten, the kind of friends I could go to their houses and sleep over. Aristotle says for friendship to exist you need bodies in the same place at the same time. Yes, he is probably right.

We drive to an antiques mart, and a smiling, roly-poly woman invites us in. She looks hungry. She looks like she would prefer her merchandise not leave the shop. Lace and silver check in but they don't check out. She fingers Belle's earrings, and another woman appraises the clothes. They want time to deliberate, so Carrie and I go for coffee, and in the café she says, "You handle it." I say, "Fine." I say, "How much will you settle for?" She gives me a number and says, "You negotiate." I say, "Okay."

Back at the store, the roly-poly woman is naming figures. I see her licking her chops, and I am upping the price when Carrie hears a number she likes and ends the deal. I say nothing although I am disappointed. The woman writes Carrie a check, and in the car she says, "Last week I couldn't talk, so this is progress."

When I look back on my life, it is the entrances and exits I remember. Moving is moving away. Richard says, "How come you can be flexible anywhere but in Arizona? How come you can plop yourself at an artist colony and feel okay in five minutes?" He is saying, "I am afraid you will leave me." He is saying, "You should leave if you are unhappy." I say, "At an artist colony there are no demands or interruptions." This isn't strictly speaking true. The last time I was at a colony a noisy writer lived underneath me, and we had words. Most of the time, though, I arrive at one of these places, tack a few postcards on a corkboard, and arrange the furniture a little to my liking. It doesn't take much. I don't notice the dirt and marks on the walls. This place isn't where I live, and so it feels like home. I don't need a special friend, although one invariably materializes. Still, if colonies were my whole existence, I would feel bereft. Colonies pretty much were my existence before Richard.

With us it is always, "Do you love me as I am?" And the answer is, "Yes and no." We are of two minds. We half believe. The other day, we were in the walk-in closet off our bedroom, looking at ties. Richard was wearing a shirt with lavender and blue stripes. Most of his ties are striped, so I suggested he wear a solid tie, and he said, "Don't make me wear the bar mitzvah tie." He has gotten it into his head that a pearly pink tie is for bar mitzvahs and weddings. He thinks the shirt will sprout ruffles and everyone will look at him. Everyone looks at him no matter what he wears because he is attractive. No one notices what anyone wears, because they are thinking about themselves.

My friend Catherine says, "You two will always fight." I say, "I have no plan B." Catherine says, "Plan A is plan B." She is a poet.

Richard has a colleague named Jackson, and they are rethinking the nature of museums. One night Jackson brings a visiting artist to dinner at our house. She, too, is English, and she has been lecturing at the university. She moves into a neighborhood, plants a garden with the residents, and after the food is harvested she stages a giant dinner party where everyone mingles. That is her art. She perches at the kitchen counter with a sleepy face and asks Richard about his insulin pump. Richard is a type 1 diabetic and needs insulin to stay alive. She asks where the device enters his body and if it hurts to insert it.

He says he inserts the catheter into his abdomen with a spring-loaded device he shows her. A thin tube of plastic with a fine needle inside is embedded under the skin. When he pulls out the needle, the tube stays in. He says it doesn't hurt, although sometimes it does, and I wonder why he conceals this, and I suppose it is because, being English, he feels he is not supposed to complain or burden others with the prickly parts of his life. I suspect, too, he wants to minimize the disease to himself. The visiting artist is a beauty with a big smile. She asks if her questions are rude. I say, "We like rude questions." She asks if I have children, and I say I do not, and my stomach drops, like missing a step, and I feel I have misplaced the instruction to reproduce.

As a kid in Long Beach, I would settle in the den beside the room divider and study the butterflies and bits of wheat pressed into the plastic. The den was a small room, where we gathered at night. The larger living room, with its curved, champagne-colored couch, was a ghost town. My mother would read the *Post* as we watched *Have Gun—Will Travel*, *Alfred Hitchcock*, and *The Twilight Zone*, the four of us bathed in the flickering light. Alone in the house, I would play *Take Five* on the stereo and dance around, imagining our small house was expanding. Rooms would open down a corridor. I would discover a new wing through a closet, and as I remember this reverie I see it is the house where I live now.

Jackson and Richard discuss museums as laboratories for social change. We drink margaritas, and the visiting artist falls asleep on the couch. I cover her with a blanket and look around. A bouquet of lilies shoots up from a bucket with a brass rim. I was at a yard sale when I leaned in too close to a space heater. I heard a sizzle like insects being electrocuted, and a horrible smell filled the air along with confetti bits of my hair. The couple, on lawn chairs, looked on in horror. The man said, "Take the bucket." I said, "Thank you."

A planter sits in the corner. I spotted it from my car, out near the curb beside a jumble of crumpled sheets. A large, robin's-egg-blue planter, Matisse-blue, conjuring the Mediterranean, palm fronds, red parrots. A woman was on the driveway, looking into the middle distance. Beside her was her husband, with a melancholy stubble on his cheeks. They scanned their possessions as if watching them sail away. They did not know where they were heading next. A little boy zoomed up to me, brandishing a blue plastic iguana, hoping to scare me away.

Richard says, "Don't try to fix me." I say, "It's not your job to calm my fears." In the dream, the driver is a stranger. The driver is a friend. We have forgotten something and have to return to the house. We sit on the porch. The mountain is far away. We are never going to reach it. We are skiing, and wind cuts my cheeks. The edges of my skis knife the hard-packed snow, and my breath softs the air. My nose is cold. A hat is pulled over my ears, and suddenly I hear a click like the sound of a mahjong tile dropping into place, and I realize you do not need to understand. All you have to do is ski down the mountain. To turn you have to unweight from the downhill ski. You have to flatten your skis in a scary way for a moment before edging again. You have to let the mountain take you to feel falling as flying.

At the artist colony where I met Richard, he was writing essays about museums, and I was writing stories, and one day he came to the door of the computer room, where I was sending emails, and he stepped over the threshold, and his gaze bounced off the shabby corners of the chairs, and I thought I had willed this, and I was afraid.

We are in Richard's studio in our house, and he says, "I don't like these pictures." He means photographs I have placed on his desk. He says, "You like these pictures." I put them somewhere else and say, "Can we organize your closet?" He says, "Okay." Inside the closet are boxes from our move six months ago. The boxes have flaps hanging out like the tongues of dogs. We throw some things away, stack file cabinets inside the closet, and place his electric keyboard against a wall. Afterward, we hike along a dusty trail and pass boulders that have taken ten thousand years to roll from point A to point B. They make you think about big time and big space, and we sit under a paloverde tree, and I say, "How much do you like your closet now?" He says, "Twenty-three out of a hundred," and I think that is a good number.

On the bed, he says, "Do you think we have the same color eyes?" I say, "Yours are brown and mine are hazel." He says, "You think your eyes are a more interesting color." Sunlight is streaming in. I say, "I can't actually see the color of your

My Life as an Animal

eyes." He says, "Tell me what you remember," and I realize there are things you see all the time that do not stick. I say, "I like the ironic glint in your eyes and their heavy lids. They look Chinese." He smiles. I say, "You are beautiful." He says, "I haven't heard that often." He says, "I don't think Suzanne thought I was beautiful." Suzanne is his ex-wife. In the bathroom, I pull back my cheeks, and he says, "You are trying to make yourself look like you've had a face-lift." I say, "Yes," and he says, "You are prettier than Coco." Coco was at our house for dinner the night before. Coco is thirty-seven and six feet tall with an arc of wild tendrils diving this way and that. She is at the top of her game, and I am sixty-four, and I say, "When I was her age," and he says, "I see you."

After my mother had open-heart surgery, my sister and I flanked her bed, urging her to live. It was as if we were waiting for a secret to be revealed. When she woke up, she said, "I want to know the truth." Then she said, "Did I shit?" "Forgiveness," says the poet Buddy Wakefield, "is the release of all hope for a better past."

Richard says, "This story is a jumble of impressions. You need a plot." I say, "What if the story is about a woman who is furnishing a house in order to see if it can be a home and in the process realizes she is not capable of feeling settled?" He says, "You are not looking for a home but a place in the world." I say, "You are right," and I am happy because, really, what is better than being known?

ELEVATOR

I was in an elevator. In one mirror my face looked like a landscape seen from a plane. In another mirror I looked like a thief who has stumbled upon unguarded jewels. The elevator stopped. Across from the door sat two men and two women on an upholstered bench. Slowly one person rose and entered the elevator. They entered one at a time. I was saying to myself, "Come on, get on with it." I was wearing a long scarf that hung to my knees. After the four were inside, the door closed, and we reached the ground. The strangers filed out silently, and I was left alone under a sky dense with stars and bright with moonlight. I moved along a road, casting a shadow that looked like I was walking on stilts. Suddenly I looked down and saw my scarf had been loosely knotted in four places. Each stranger had tied the scarf while my attention was directed elsewhere. When I realized magic could fall upon you like a breath or a kiss, even if you arranged life to steal away such moments, I felt a thrill move through me, red and slithery, and I stopped in my tracks.

SIXTY

I am at Yaddo, the artist colony in Saratoga Springs. It is
my sixtieth birthday, and Suzy, my photographer friend, says,
"Stretch toward people you don't like." What do I have to
lose? Really, I have nothing to lose. Suzy says, "Don't exert
your will, just play through." At breakfast I sit with a man and
a woman I usually avoid. They are careful. It's as if Charlie
Rose can hear them in Manhattan and their writing futures
depend on maintaining an inscrutable front. Today I listen to
them, and their remarks sound like koans you could embroi-
der on a pillow: "Hearing is the last thing to go." "Gravity is
a force not well understood." Oddly, I feel lighter.

As if Suzy has set in motion a chain reaction, Richard
invites me for a walk. Usually after breakfast he strides off
by himself along wooded paths that snake the gigantic rich-
people's estate where Yaddo is set. The day I arrive, I spot
a man in a little parlor off the dining room, a slender man
with salt-and-pepper hair who looks autumnal in brown and
gray gear except for the fancy, rectangular glasses he wears
with flashes of orange and blue. He has a musical English
voice and eyes that smile, although often they sit catlike
and watchful behind his specs. Human beings have an on-

off switch that says, You, yes; you, no. We smell each other and mirror neurons fire. Richard is married. He does not say much about his wife, but he is married.

Yet we are similar, we find, as we talk at meals: not depressed but not all that alive. He says at seventeen he married a girl from his village, believing the baby she was carrying was his. "Or I felt responsible, or I wanted sex on a regular basis." He shrugs. They were not in love, and Marilyn wasn't faithful, and when their son was three Richard left, and he and Trevor, now a grown man, do not speak. Richard is unguarded, and I see his sorrow, and the story attracts me because he has saved himself but not escaped the consequences. Trevor is owed an apology, Richard feels, although he has not offered one. "Isn't there still time?" I ask, and he shoots me a grumpy smile.

The day before my birthday, my friend Natalie and her daughter drive to Yaddo from Massachusetts. Natalie and I have been friends since our Barnard days. Kate Millett was our teacher. She brought us together. Natalie's daughter is twenty and at college, an artist—a gorgeous vegan spawn of the women's movement. Natalie was one of the cool, slouchy girls who wrote poetry and rode motorcycles and magnetized Kate. In the early 1970s, when *Sexual Politics* made Kate a star and she was outed as a lesbian, Natalie had an affair with Kate's husband, Fumio, a Japanese sculptor, and they traveled together to Sweden. Later, Natalie kicked aside her motorcycle and went to law school.

We drive to a bar and order margaritas. As a present she gives me a photograph of Kate and Fumio from the time we were all close. They are on a bed, Fumio in the back, cross-legged and taking up no space. "Little bird," Kate used to call him. In the photograph, he could be a child, but if you look closely at his unsmiling face, you see he is not young and that

My Life as an Animal

he is a storage unit. As a boy during World War II, his job was clearing bodies out of Hiroshima. Kate is in the foreground, leaning on an elbow, wearing a long white shirt and dark slacks. She takes up space, and her eyes are sad. She is already famous in the way Andy Warhol calls a commodity. Kate and Fumio are our older artist friends, and they are luminous, the improbable mating of the boy marked by history and the fleshy odalisque on a mission to reroute history. I love them. I thank Natalie.

Richard and I walk into the cool morning air, and we are alone on the paths strewn with fallen leaves. We circle four small lakes and our jackets swish, nearly touching. I am used to being alone and I like solitude, but existence without intimacy is dull and flat. Richard is describing his early days in New York City when he would order eggs over easy at a diner on Columbus Avenue. Every day the waiter would bring porridge or waffles because no one could understand his accent. He would eat the food anyway, and I see him, too polite to send it back, and I like his forbearance and idiocy. I say, "It's my birthday," but I do not say which one, although I think he can tell because a tear plops down my cheek. If you think there is a part of you that makes you unlovable, you will protect it like your child and show it to everyone. We walk until we arrive at rose beds set out like the gardens of a French palace. The branches are pruned, although a few bold blossoms persist.

A few days before our walk, Richard has visited my studio to read some of his work. I have made a fire and placed flowers in a vase. He sits on the couch with his computer on his lap. I sit across from him and look at his hair in the flickering light. In one of the stories he reads, he is twenty-one, working in Birmingham in a dead-end, clerk job. He has left his marriage to Marilyn and is earning barely enough money for food and the tiny room he rents in a ramshackle house owned by a couple called the Mulvaneys. One afternoon Richard wanders into a museum and furtively eats a sandwich in front of a painting by John Millais. The picture's vibrant colors and message of hope, set against the backdrop of the soot-blackened city, seem to speak to him directly. He has already met the woman he will live with next. She is at university, and he begins to study and in time is accepted, too.

The story is part of a book he is writing about how meaning is constructed in museums and how space is interpreted wherever there are signs, even those marking a wildlife trail, for example. In another piece he reads, he talks about display as a widening circle of identification, including the history of human display, from gladiatorial contests, to slave auctions, to operating theaters, to the Paris morgue, where bodies were laid out for public inspection. He describes the plight of Ota Benga, a Pygmy man who, in 1906, was displayed in the Monkey House at the Bronx Zoo. Benga, unable to return to his home in the Belgian Congo, killed himself ten years after his release. I can see these spectacles, each a site of melancholy and fascination, and I wonder if there will ever come a time when we will not want to look. I tell Richard his writing is alive and that I can enter his world. He laughs, and light glistens on his teeth.

At the artist colony we are fourteen in all, quite the little microcosm of ages and personalities, and we take to playing a parlor game called Mafia in which someone randomly draws a card that appoints them a hit man. I am routinely the first to be suspected and killed off. When I ask people why, they say, "You look guilty." Richard, on the other hand, is trusted, although often he is the killer. At the end of his stay, we drive

My Life as an Animal

to the airport and can't find the entrance. He says, "It's a sign I shouldn't leave."

HAVE YOU EVER WISHED TO SPEND YOUR LIFE IN AN airport, presenting your shampoo vials to security guards, slipping your laptop from its case, arriving at your gate, only to learn your flight has been delayed? You float above the ground, rocking on a glassy pond.

One morning at Yaddo, I wake up with an idea: consciousness and religion arrived together, the one mistaken for the other. I picture a gracile primate wandering across a savanna. Hearing hooves approach, she looks for a tree to escape into but can find none. She registers the understanding in her head. She *hears* a thought, and it must feel like a voice originating from another source, a power greater than the animal and outside her. I want to share this idea, and the next thing I know Richard is in my head. We cross paths in the little parlor lined with books. There are throw pillows on the sofa and chairs, although they are straight backed and uncomfortable. At first his hands rest on his thighs, and then he picks up a black stone with white stripes someone has brought back from a hike. It is smooth as skin, and he rubs it absently. "Can you picture her?" I ask. He says, "Picture her, I am her," and he talks about the numinous—moments, like our awareness of death, that are terrifying and fascinating at the same time. I am lost in the conversation, although I do not show how much.

At the bar with Natalie, Joni Mitchell sings about love from both sides of life. She says she can still fall in love, even though love dies, and I tell Natalie I have met a man. She pulls her fingers through her thick curls and says, "Your life is still defined by men." I think she is wrong, and I think she is right. I think a kiss can be a detour and a kiss can awaken your mind. Natalie is the kind of girl I would jump out of a window to impress, but there is no window. She says, "Maya's generation, the girls don't operate that way." I think, If that is true, it is because we made it possible for them. If you suddenly wake me from sleep and say, "What is the thing you are most proud of in your life?" I will say, "The women's movement and the way it changed the world."

I AM ON A TRAIN A YEAR LATER AND RUN INTO A woman I slightly know. I tell her about Richard, and she says, "How could you let him leave his wife?" When Richard returned to Arizona, he told Suzanne he had met someone, and he moved out. For six months I shuttled between New York and Phoenix, seeing if we could make it work. Richard says he did not leave his marriage for me. He says Yaddo cracked him open. We believe what we believe.

The woman on the train does not sound judgmental, more like a naturalist asking a scorpion how pincers work. I say, "Richard decided," but she knows I did not put a gun to his head, and I know I did not say, "Stop," because he might have listened to me.

We get what we want more often than we remember because we keep changing our minds.

ANDRÉ

My sister and I are at Starbucks in the New Jersey town where she lives. My sister is the keeper of the family lore, now that our parents are dead. I do not know how she knows what she knows. People trust her. She sells real estate and has one of those I-will-listen faces. When our mother was alive, my sister would squeeze her like an orange to get at her secrets. Ellen is smiling and shaking her head, as if remembering, in itself, is a joy.

We are leaning on the little round table, and I can see the girl my sister was. I see her at camp with her silky ponytail, fuzzy sweaters, and short shorts. Girls liked her. Everyone liked my sister. She says, "Zev fucked everybody." She means our father's brother. Zev the furrier with the Clark Gable smile, Zev who lived in a ten-room apartment on Park Avenue, Zev with the gleaming black hair. Ellen taps my arm, and a light comes into her eyes, "Zev fucked Bell." She means our mother's younger sister. Aunt Bell was tan and wiry, thinner than our mother. In the Long Beach years, Toby packed on a little padding, but never Bell. She was a stringy, tendony thing you would have to pull out of your teeth if you ate her.

31

According to Ellen, our father's brother meets our mother's sister at a wedding both families attend, and during the festivities Zev and Bell arrange to meet. I see the hotel. I see a bar in the lobby and martinis on a silver tray. There are thick towels in the white-tiled bathroom, a vase of pink roses beside the bed. Bell has a husband who does not speak. No one remembers a word out of his mouth. She has a daughter who skulks around with angry circles under her eyes and a son who disappears like invisible ink when he leaves a room. Zev kisses Bell. They are on the bed after sex. She showers. He calls to her as he dresses, a laugh in his voice, and says, "Stay as long as you like, darling." People pay so much for his furs he can live forever on the profits, except he gambles away his money and dies young of a heart attack. "What heart attack?" my father says when I tell him the news, his lips trembling. "It was a mob hit made to look like a heart attack. They have drugs. He owed money."

In my favorite memory of Zev, he strides along the boardwalk in Long Beach, looking like a movie star in his thousand-dollar, camel's hair coat. Another brother of my father's has settled here along with my grandfather, who lives in a beachfront hotel with his third wife. My grandfather gazes at the surf with the still, satisfied expression of a chimp with a cigar. My father and Zev foot the bills for their *tata*, the former pants presser. When Zev is in Long Beach, we bounce behind him in a Fellini parade. The air smells like the Mediterranean.

In my sister's memory of Zev, she is nineteen and recuperating from an abortion at the apartment of Zev and his wife, Kate. While Ellen is sleeping, she feels a body beside her. Zev has slid under the covers and is pushing his penis against her behind. She is bloody and tired, and she tells him to go away. He drags himself out of the bed and slinks off. In Starbucks, as she tells the story, she is laughing. She is sixty-six with diamonds on both hands, and our uncle has been wearing cement galoshes for thirty years.

I say, "What the hell?" Ellen shrugs and puts out her palms. Her eyebrows rise, and she laughs. My story, too, concerns a girl and a bed, only the man is not an uncle but the family shrink, the guru who treated my mother, my sister, me, and other members of our family. We were part of a cult of sorts, a gaggle of rich, unschooled Jews under the influence of a smart man, a doctor, a sad man, a lonely man, a fat man, an ugly man, a man who knew things and loved the people he treated or needed them or took them for all they were worth.

His name was André, and when Ellen and I look back, André rises like the moon, a red moon with melancholy eyes. I see his face. Not exactly. Fifty years have passed since I last laid eyes on him, standing in a doorway in a silk robe. The tasseled sash was hanging down on both sides of his big belly.

Here are some things I know about André: He earned a medical degree in France, where he trained as a psychoanalyst. He fled Europe in 1942 to escape the Nazis. He published essays in analytic journals, and authors in the field inscribed books to him. You can Google him, André Glaz.

When I was fourteen, André took me into his bed. I was visiting him in the country, and he came to the back garden, where I was watching birds. The birds were splashing in a fountain when he called me inside. He put his hands on my breasts and inside my underpants. It was afternoon. It was fall. A hazy sun was softening the air. The second time he took me to his bed he told me to touch him. He was fat and jowly. Eventually I said no. I said no in the voice of a sleepy child. I said, "I'm tired and I want to go to sleep." I was not tired. It was 1961.

André entered our lives in 1958, when my sister was seventeen and I was eleven and she returned from college under mysterious circumstances. It turned out she had stolen a wallet from a girl in her dorm and left it out on her dresser. My parents kept it secret. I listened through walls, like Polonius. When Ellen came home, Zev was in treatment with André for "mood swings." André was also treating Kate, and her and Zev's two daughters, one of whom did not eat. Also in treatment was another, lower-echelon uncle. After my sister started seeing André, my mother entered treatment, and three years later it was my turn.

André liked to say, "If someone insists, 'One and one equal three,' say, 'Okay, one and one equal three.' What's the skin off your nose?" He told my sister she could not "swim with barracudas." He called her "kid." He said, "Kid, you are not equipped." He encouraged my mother to study literature and art. She enrolled in courses at the New School. One professor had a thick accent she could not understand, and my mother was disheartened. André said, "Keep listening, do not quit, it will become easier." She listened. It became easier. He urged her to travel on her own, and she left us for a month to visit Europe for the first time. André was the one who paid for my sister's abortion and kept her secret from our parents. He guided Ellen and other patients on a trip around the world. There she is in a snapshot, grinning in front of the Taj Mahal. There she is in front of a sphinx with her hand on a slim hip.

During my sessions with André, he seemed bored. I don't blame him. I wanted whatever my sister was getting. I liked wandering around Manhattan on my own. I would sit in a little café near André's office on Madison Avenue and watch couples exchange knowing looks over the rims of coffee cups. I would order coffee. I did not drink coffee.

A few months into my sessions, André invited me to Cold Spring, and I felt like I was headed somewhere. I remember fourteen. Everything tastes good. And you could kiss boys in crevices along the black jetties that stabbed the waves. You and a boy could kiss, and the salt of the kiss and the salt of the waves would lodge forever in your mind. On the train to Cold Spring, I imagined books André would recommend and wooded trails we would walk, speaking of seriousness played out on cobbled streets. André summoned me to his bed before Zev and Kate arrived, and I rose to the ceiling as if to get a better look.

Have you ever left your body? People talk about this happening during trauma. Maybe it is a throwback to our chimpy past, when the endangered primate searched for a tree to climb into at the sound of pounding hooves. I looked down at a girl in a blue cardigan with her arms by her sides. Next to her was an old man with a beach ball belly and wispy white hair. He circled my nipples and asked if it felt good. His breaths grew faster. I smelled his cigar.

I want to remember André's bed. He formed me. Not really. He is a knot in my shoulder. He made me the way a baker makes bread in a bowl and lets it rise, and punches it down, and forms it in a pan and scores the top with little notches of cunning and indifference. When I see shadows graffitied onto brick walls, smoky, shadowy forms that look like they are coming for you as you round a corner, I see André.

At his house that night, I sat on a blue velvet couch as the sleeping arrangements were announced. When I was assigned to André's bed, my aunt must have seen a cloud cross my eyes. She smiled and waved her red fingernails, saying,

"Phoebe sleeps with André all the time." She meant her youngest child. Kate was a stunning redhead in the style of Rita Hayworth with skin as soft as a moth's wing. Phoebe was twelve. What did she think was happening in André's bed?

He was bolder the second time, and I felt aroused. I felt like an actor without lines who has to stay onstage until the scene ends. André asked me to touch him, and that was the edge. Slowly I told myself to stop this. Time was slow. I said, "I'm tired and I want to go to sleep." He rolled off me and slipped away. I do not know where he slept.

The next day he did not look at me. Before I left, he took me aside and said, "Don't tell your mother." He did not mention my father. His head was at an angle, as if he were looking at a painting behind me on the wall. A painting of a girl with a wide mouth, a girl in a field of wildflowers with the expression of a cow or a sheep, a painting by Renoir. I wondered if Long Beach would still be there when I got off the train, and when it was, I saw life goes on and you don't have anywhere else to go.

I told no one. After André touched me, I could not tell if I wanted to be touched by everyone but him. A few weeks later I stopped seeing him. Maybe it was his idea.

Ellen says, "Daddy loaned André money. He lost it in the stock market and didn't pay it back. Daddy didn't ask for it. Mom was the one who got it from André." I say, "How?" She says, "At the end of one of her sessions, she just asked for it." I see my mother in a chair, wearing a teal-blue suit from Bergdorf's. She prefers to think about the money than the kind of person André is. She does not meet his eyes. She does not look people in the eye. She speaks to the air beside him, and he rises from the desk where he sits between trips to the kitchen for food and writes her a check she carries home in triumph and with other emotions she has taken to her grave. (Actually, a copper urn.)

Ellen says, "Mom was finished with André before he died." I say, "When did he die?" She says he died of a heart attack in 1968 or 1969. I remember my mother calling me with the news. She sounded sad. Maybe she was crying. She was smoking. I heard her inhale several times as if the smoke was hard to swallow. Ellen says, "Mom blamed him for telling her not to see her mother before she died. She always regretted that." I say, "Why blame André? She was the one who listened to him." Ellen says, "You're right, but she blamed him anyway." Ellen breaks off a piece of cookie that has sat untouched. She pops it in her mouth and says, "But that's not what finished him in her eyes. It was when Zev and Kate needed money. Their business was in trouble from Zev's gambling, and André said to Mom, 'A good sister-in-law helps out.' Mom said to him, 'There is preferred stock, and there is common stock, and to you we are common stock.' She walked out and never went back."

I say, "Wow." I am silent for a moment. I say, "I wish she had walked out for me." My sister takes my hand and leans forward. I do not want the parts of my life erased. Ellen says, "She would have if she had known." I try to imagine a mother like this, but no picture forms. I did not tell my mother about André because I thought she would think I was lying. I thought she would think I was hurting someone she loved.

At seventeen, I returned to André. I don't know why, but I can see the members of my family, and they are loving him, and I can see myself outside. When I looked at him, I could see the bed. I see it now, the window that looks out to the back yard. The fountain where birds are chirping. A

André   37

cello concerto is sweeping out the window as he calls me inside.

Before I returned to André, he sent me two articles he had published in the psychoanalytic journal *American Imago*. He was proud of them. One concerns *Hamlet*, the other is titled "Iago or Moral Sadism." I still have them. One is signed, "To Laurie, André G." I have occasionally read them over the years, and each time I am surprised by their sensitivity. He must have had something, and in some sense I don't mind this. Maybe I even like it. In the piece on *Othello*, he references Dostoyevsky, Pascal, Flaubert, and other writers. At fourteen, I had not known people who read these authors. By the time I was seventeen, my parents had moved back to Manhattan and I was wandering around the Village, slipping into art films and steamy cafés. Maybe I wanted André to see this.

His first language was Polish. In addition to English and French, he knew Russian, German, and Italian. He spoke with a thick accent, but his writing is conversational and speculative. Considering Iago, he seems strangely self-revealing, as if he is trying to come clean: "What revolts us is the fact that Iago looks like a human being and behaves like a beast. What revolts us is that he looks like ourselves and yet he does not act as we would act. Or maybe he reminds us of our own cannibalism, cruelty, and destructiveness, that we shy away from him. We do not like such a distorted image of our own inner self. Most probably that is the reason why we do not believe the masochists or the victims when they describe what has happened to them. I do not know if God was created in our image, but I am sure the devil is in our likeness."

André and I did not speak about the weekend at his house. It was as if it had not happened. At the time I was seeing a boy, and one night the boy and I were in my room and my parents woke up and banged on the door. After the boy and I found our clothes and smoothed the sheets, we came into the living room and saw my parents huddled like actors in a farce or a melodrama. I mean, it could have gone either way. My father said to the boy, "You are no longer welcome here," and I left with the boy. That is how I remember it. The boy and I walked uptown, and I was scared and excited, as if my life were beginning. I don't know what time it was, and I did not call André to say I was on my way. I wanted him to help me the way he had helped my sister.

I rode the elevator up to his floor and rang the bell, and after a while, he came to the door in a maroon bathrobe, his stomach pressing against the silk, his hair messed. His mouth was turned down, and he looked like he was witnessing a pileup on a road. He said, "Don't ever do this again, come here unannounced." He sounded weary and confused. He closed the door, and I looked at the little peephole in the center, wanting to peer in but afraid I would meet his eye. I went down to where the boy was waiting, and that was the last time I saw André.

Ellen says, "He had the thickest lips I've ever seen." She shudders and laughs. I say, "What was going on with these men, getting into bed with young girls?" She says, "They knew they could get away with it." She puts her hands behind her head and leans back. "Zev told André *I* was the one who seduced *him*. Can you believe it? He was scared I would say something, so he went to his protector. André confronted me, and I said, 'Are you out of your mind? Why would I want that limp dick between my legs?' André said, 'All right, all right, calm down, kid, but you know, he's a very sick man.'"

André   39

I say, "I think André was infatuated with Zev. Maybe we all were." Ellen says, "André knew a good thing when he had it. He drained all Daddy's cash. Daddy used to keep the cash he made from selling coats 'to the street' on Saturdays. André got it all. Fifty thousand dollars. That would be like half a million today." I say, "Why did Daddy do it?" I see our father's soft smile. She says, "He would have done anything if he thought it would help his family."

She leans in and says, "I think André was evil, but he taught me things." I say, "What did he teach you?" She says, "He taught me to stand back and observe. He taught me to understand who I was up against in the world. He said, 'Ellen, people will try to take you down. Trust your gut. Your gut will tell you where you are safe.'"

I say, "In his world there were barracudas and fish who could swim away. That's all." She says, "I needed to understand that. You were stronger, more like Mom." I say, "I didn't think the world was dangerous," and as I say these words I remember the way my mother would sometimes stroke my arm gently and say, "Don't be afraid. Don't be like me. Don't be afraid of anything."

SEVERAL YEARS AGO, RICHARD AND I VISITED A friend in Maine, and while we were there our friend invited a man and a woman to dinner. The woman was a therapist, part of what she called "the recovery movement," and she quickly reported having had an affair with her analyst when she was twenty-six. Two years later the analyst broke it off, and the experience set her life on its course. It was her story, and she told it like a performer reciting a practiced monologue. Richard said, "Laurie had a sexual experience with her analyst as well." I thought, I did? Then I thought, Oh yes,

André. Richard was throwing the woman a fish so she would not feel alone.

The woman and her companion were friends or sometimes a couple. The man had been quiet until André was mentioned. He had intense eyes and an enigmatic smile. His belly was round, his hair thinning, his arms and legs untoned, despite his work as a landscape gardener. We were drinking margaritas and eating chips. Sailboats raced outside the windows, and I looked around my friend's peaceful loft with its large, abstract paintings, couches by a window, a coffee table made from an old, green door. I was on a stool and once or twice rubbed my shoulder. The man said, "Can I give you a massage? I have studied massage." I said, "Okay." My mother used to say, "Nothing is free." I did not want her to be right. The man stood too close as he worked on my neck. Softly, he said, "Does it feel good?" I said, "Yes." He kept working. I closed my eyes. I didn't like him. His hands were soothing. He was silent for a while and then he said, "Can I kiss your shoulder? These shoulders don't know they are loved." I did not want the kiss. I thought he was ugly. I said, "Okay," and I felt his lips, cool and quick, on my skin.

That night in bed Richard said, "Why did you let him kiss you?" I said, "It felt easier than saying no." Richard said, "When you talked about André, he thought he had found another victim. I'm sorry I got you into it." I said, "You didn't. The Pauls of the world and the Lauries of the world will always find each other." Richard said, "The same thing for the first time." And André was in the attic room. The ceiling was so low we could touch it from the bed. André was behind his desk looking bored and chomping hearts of palm, trying to lose weight. Suffering does not ennoble people. Suffering mostly crushes people.

André   41

I recently received a phone call from a woman whose family, too, had been members of André's cult in the same years my family was. She had read something I had written and found my number. She said all the members of her family had been André's patients, including her parents, an aunt and uncle (glamorous and rich), their children, and more. André had had sex with all the females, including the caller, who was four at the time. As she spoke, I felt as if an alien had shown up at my door, confirming the existence of other planets. She seemed surprised I was more interested in who André was than aggrieved by what he had done. She told me the date he emigrated from France. She said he purported and may even have believed the sex he engaged in was therapeutic.

I remember the excitement of being so young adults loomed like giants, and you wanted them big as the moon so they could shed light on you. I remember stumbling upon knowledge I could not unstitch. A bed, sunlight streaming in at a sharp angle, a life divided into two parts. Or not divided. The bed is as vivid as the happiest moments of my childhood, running on the beach with my best friend and her dog. The dog had tawny fur and looked like a small deer. I wonder who André thought I was. I do not think he gave me much thought at all.

SPY

Heddy's boyfriend and I would run into each other at parties and want to slap each other's faces and jump into bed. I thought that was how people were, and I felt in step with something. I had not seen Heddy for fifteen years, and there she was, on the other side of a salad bar on Broadway. Her hair was long and blond as it had been in the days when she had been one of the Joni Mitchells at Claire's. She said she was caring for someone sick. She did not mention Jerry. Maybe Jerry was sick and no one was supposed to know. They had been famous for a while in the performance art scene, telling stories about their life using with mice and mazes. I thought Heddy and Jerry would always be together, and it was exciting to think a tie could come undone. Heddy struck me as a woman of mystery. She was spooning hummus over lettuce in a plastic container, and I wondered if she had become a spy. She resembled a spy on a TV show I was watching. The spy had been in retirement and was working in a flower shop when her son was kidnapped in France and she had to fly to his rescue. It turned out she could ride motorcycles and pilot helicopters. She could speak Russian and Arabic. She traded sex for information and blew people's heads off. Seeing Heddy apart from Jerry, I wished I had always been interested in the girlfriends of the men I had known. Sex and violence had obscured my view of them, and to make up for this I gave Heddy a life consisting entirely of violence and sex.

TOBY DEAD

At eighty-nine, my mother learns her arteries are clogged with plaque like tubes with toothpaste. She brushes off the news and goes into cardiac arrest. A squat little machine that looks like R2-D2 is attached to her by a vacuum cleaner hose, and my sister is holding a clipboard. Ellen is tapping the clipboard with a long, hard fingernail saying, "You have two choices, Ma, sign the form or dead. Which is it, Ma, the form or dead?" I am glancing from the machine to my mother, who looks like a chimp caught in a lab experiment. She trains her beady eyes on Ellen, as if she is being conned, but she takes the pen in her monkey paw and signs on for three more years of life—as well as a stroke and the twenty-four-hour care of home aides. My mother and I do not get along, do not see eye to eye, but love is somewhere in the room. I feel responsible for her no matter what. It's like watching your own death.

The last time I see her she is a pile of sticks on a hospital bed. I enter her room, and she shouts, "Get away from me." Her voice is loud, and the woman in the next bed pleads with me to stop her. "How?" I say, "I am open to suggestions."

We don't pick who we love. We don't pick who we don't love. People say, "I am sorry for your loss." What is my loss?

When I am thirty-five and my father is dying of liver cancer, my mother sends me to the hospital to see him off, and when she arrives says, "You killed him." At nineteen, on the way to my marriage to a young man named Bruce, my mother says to me, "Go get killed." Why? Bruce's parents have invited some friends to the ceremony, and my mother is against this.

Everyone has stories. Some people let go of them like stones from their pockets. Some people keep them because it's what they have.

When I am small and crossing streets, my mother and I squeeze hands in little pulse beats. It means, "I love you." We live in Washington Heights, near St. Nicholas Avenue, and it is a river of shops and strangers. Foreign words, sausages wrapped in greasy wax paper and eaten on the fly. We are moving, and we are together. My sister is at school. My father is at work. And Toby and I are on the streets. People talk to us. Strangers talk to my mother. She is beautiful with deep-set eyes and high cheekbones, clip-clopping in spike heels and pencil skirts, and there is something about her. She says more than she needs to. She prefers strangers to other people. Strangers on buses, at the Automat, in the park. She can say anything she wants. What can it hurt? In the morning, I watch from her bed as she drifts around naked, splashing on My Sin and attaching nylons to dangling garters. She will take me to the park to shovel sand, but it's the streets she's after, and she is waiting for Ellen to reappear. You can tell they are married by the looks they exchange in the school yard and by the way they laugh at things I still will not understand by the time Toby is dead and I am sixty-one.

When I am five, I go to sleep-away camp for two months. I miss my parents. I am happy. I pass the test for swimming in deep water. After lunch, I find my mother's postcards fanned

My Life as an Animal

out on my bed. Her handwriting is neat, and I see her face floating up to the rafters, and I look into her eyes, wondering if she can see me on my blanket, pulled taut for inspection. She writes, "Learn to do everything. There is nothing you cannot do." Crickets chirp outside. An indolent fly buzzes a window. My happiest memories of my mother are memories of missing her.

When I am seven, we move to Long Beach full-time. We have dinners out. My father likes restaurants. I feel his arm around my shoulder in the car, on walks. At the Chinese restaurant, he shares food with my sister and me. My mother eats her own portion of roast pork with Chinese vegetables. The vegetables are bok choy, but we do not know their name. Long Beach is not a city. You have to drive from point A to point B. When my father and sister are gone, I will go anywhere with my mother, even though I cannot tell if she is happy or unhappy. We prowl shopping malls, where there are stores and strangers but no streets. She wants to get lost. I adore her. She embarrasses me. She will say someone is ugly when they are close enough to hear. I want to look like her. I spend as much time as I can at the home of my best friend.

My best friend has a dog. I want a dog. My mother says, "I didn't grow up with animals." She means she came from poverty, where there wasn't room to house a pet or money to feed one. She means she is urban and animals are part of the mysterious realm of farms and woods—sinister, vacant places where beasts can feed on you and you on them. She complains about the dirt and hair animals leave around, but really she is afraid. She covers it with talk. She speaks to me like a used car salesman trying to unload a clunker, and that voice goes into me with so little resistance I use it whenever I want something.

The Toby of Long Beach is backing up a finned, yellow Plymouth, looking over her shoulder with a cigarette twisted in her lips. We are headed to the Malibu Beach Club, and I am fat. In a home movie, Toby sits outside her cabana in a turquoise halter pulled up to her bronzed shoulders. In the late afternoon, she pads to the ocean, where waves lap her copper legs and foam surrounds her trim waist. Each splash is a shock because she does not know how to swim. She tells strangers about the time my father rigged a float behind a rowboat and Ellen, then a toddler, slipped out and almost drowned. To anyone on the sand she says, "My child turned blue." Her face darkens. She says, "I see it."

She says I can have a goldfish, and we name him Sylvester. He sits on the kitchen counter in a glass bowl, a single fish with a gentle smile. He ignores his ceramic bridge but darts around the fluorescent-green frond that floats on the surface and makes a racy contrast to his orange scales. I angle my face, and we watch each other through the glass.

When a snail materializes on the bottom of his bowl, my mother and I have another character to chronicle. We watch the snail grow from a speck you can't be sure is alive to a small gastropod with a curved brown shell. We call it Burt, and in time Burt is fully grown. He is Sylvester's roommate, but they are like boarders who see each other during trips to the bathroom and otherwise do not socialize.

One day Burt crawls out of the bowl. He wants to be recognized when he makes an appearance. I spot him on the kitchen counter in front of the toaster as Perry Como sings the theme song from *Picnic*. Perry is crooning about romance in ordinary life, and I wonder if Burt's venture is an example of this. His escape is unsettling, a creature setting off on his own. My mother learned to drive when we

My Life as an Animal

moved to Long Beach, but for her to equal Burt's daring she would need to barrel down to Mexico and disappear into a mountain village. On the postcards she sends, she writes, "The fish misses you."

IT IS 2007, AND TOBY SITS ACROSS FROM ME AT Starbucks, her hair fluffy and white—a color close to her former platinum bleach jobs. She is out of her wheelchair on a wooden chair, spooning up a Frappuccino and licking her lips. She says, "I never eat between meals. I am only doing it to please you." I raise the subject of money. I seldom ask her for things, but she has given Ellen her diamond ring, worth forty thousand dollars, and I am commuting to Arizona to see Richard and I want my mother to be nice to me. I propose she give me five thousand a year for four years, half the value of the ring. She narrows her eyes, and her head snaps back. She says, "I won't give you anything."

Money is what my mother has the way she used to have beauty. She likes to talk about money. I like to talk about money. I want her jewelry and the little carved bowls she sets around her apartment.

She tries to stand and cannot. She is loud, and we are getting looks. I suggest we talk about Ellen's grandchildren or the biography of Harry Truman she is reading. Why does she like Harry Truman? She doesn't think it matters he dropped the bomb. It wasn't on her people.

She squints, pushing aside her drink and reaching for her walking stick. Her good arm shakes, and her back is twisting into a C shape. I help her balance, and she leans into me, making a face. Because we are touching? Because I can walk? She instructs me on how to position my feet, move the wheelchair, lock the wheels, as if I have not performed these tasks dozens of times. The chair takes on an alien aspect, and I forget to swing aside the footrests to allow her a clear path. As she shuffles forward, she nearly falls, and we sway together like drunken lovers in a tango, like partners in a failed double act, embracing and looking daggers. It is funny, and I laugh.

When Toby laughs, her nostrils quiver and her eyes tear. One day when I was in high school she accidentally attached her sable scarf to my winter coat, and when I called her from school to say a furry snake was poking from a sleeve, she fell on the floor and said, "When did you see the snake? What did you think it was?" I told her, and then she asked me to tell her again. At Starbucks, she plops her backside onto her wheelchair and squirms. I slip my hands under her arms, feeling the soft dough of her, and hoist her up until she is settled. All the way back to her apartment, she wishes for me to be shot or run over by a car, her chin up, her voice raining down. Passersby stare. What does she care? I get a helicopter view above Fifty-Seventh Street of a shrunken old woman in a worn brown hat and her sixty-year-old daughter in need of Botox.

I ONCE EMAILED A MAN ON A DATING SITE, AND WHEN I signed my name, he wrote back, "I always thought your writing in the *Village Voice* was overrated." I didn't respond. I mean, what can you say? But the thing is, the remark went into me. I am a few months short of my sixtieth birthday, riding in a taxi to an artists' residency in Nebraska City. The driver is detailing his gastric bypass surgery and pointing out the hospital where it was performed. I am riding in a taxi from Omaha because there is no public transportation to Nebraska City, and when we pull into town, I see why. The main street looks like a mouth with missing teeth, stores framing in their windows clues to their tragic abandonments: books scattered on the floor with their spines broken, apples rotting on a table under an inch of dust, chairs overturned like beetles on their backs. It looks like me, I think, this place.

Gertrude Stein, when she didn't know if she had anything to say, before she concocted the pellucid but indecipherable style that gave away nothing as it gazed with seeming serenity at everything, before she invented herself as a fat Buddha, devised a system to divide people into two categories. You could divide anything into halves, like loaves of the brain. Stein's idea was derived from her study of psychology with William James, before she dropped out of medical school saying, "You don't know what boredom is." She thought there were people whose natural way of fighting is the attack and people whose natural way of fighting is resistance. When I read this, I thought, Toby and I, attack. Ellen and my father, resistance. My sister says she was subsumed by Toby while I got away. She says, "You got the better deal." I say, "Maybe, but you got the diamond."

DURING MY MOTHER'S LAST MONTHS, SHE SITS WITH her eyes closed, her hand propping her chin. Ellen says, "It's as if she is going to sleep, but she is thinking. She is waiting for death, like an appointment." Ellen and I are on the phone. I am in Arizona, and I imagine my mother in a waiting room, in an airport lounge or a train station, one of those bardo spaces where we contemplate arrivals and departures. Arrivals are about expectation—maybe hope, maybe dread. Departures are about looking back and summing up, even if closure exists only in stories. While departing, we glimpse the promise of our past arrivals. While arriving, we project forward to the next, looming farewell.

In December, Toby asks my sister, "When is Laurie coming?" Ellen says, "In a week." Toby says, "Then I'll have both my daughters with me." I think, Whatever she wants. What can it hurt?

WHEN TOBY IS EIGHTY-SEVEN, WE VISIT THE NEUE Galerie on Fifth Avenue. She has jumped at the suggestion to tour the museum, and I assume she understands that the artists there are German and Austrian. As we pass through rooms filled with works by Gustav Klimt, Oskar Kokoschka, Egon Schiele, Josef Hoffmann, Otto Dix, and George Grosz, Toby proclaims at top volume—although not in an ill-tempered way—that each is a Nazi. When I offer that so-and-so hadn't actually been a Nazi because the artist predated the regime, or was Jewish, or had opposed the Nazis, Toby takes this in stride, expressing neither relief nor trust in my account. I am not ruffled because earlier, at the coat check, she has broken my heart. My mother, who prides herself on being chic, has arrived in a navy peacoat. I remember when she bought it on sale eight years ago. Her eyesight is failing, and she cannot see how pilled the fabric is, how soiled and threadbare the collar and cuffs are. Underneath the coat her blouse, vest, and skirt look faded and in need of a cleaning. I say, "Ma, you can't wear that coat anymore. It's falling apart." She laughs.

She likes stories in which she loses her grip. Her favorite is about arriving at the office of her dentist just as he showed up and watching the bridge that had come loose fly out of her mouth and land on his shoe. About the coat, she says, "Go on, I'll have it cleaned, it'll be fine."

When we finish surveying the art, she wants coffee in the museum café. There is a long line, and I know the place is expensive, so to head off a scene I bring her a menu and

My Life as an Animal

report the coffee costs four fifty. "They should go get killed," she says in Yiddish, matter-of-factly, and we walk north to the Guggenheim, where we take trays and look at the food. Toby chooses a chocolate chip cookie, extracting sworn testimony from the woman behind the counter it is free of nuts. "Nuts will kill me," she says. The water for her tea is not scalding enough, so she sends it back, and after the curtain descends on this episode, we find a table and Toby withdraws two documents from her purse.

I know what they are. My sister has visited Ellis Island and brought back copies of the manifests from the ships my mother's parents sailed on to America. One says my grandfather, Chaim Bilder, departed from Rotterdam in 1899, at age eighteen. My grandmother, Pesha Baum, left from Hamburg in 1906, at seventeen. Both had lived in Poland, but their nationalities are listed as "Hebrew."

I have seen home movies of my grandfather holding me in his arms. He is smiling under a thick mustache, and his skin looks burnished under the yellow lights. I do not remember him. He died when I was one. (According to my sister, we are visiting and she makes me cry, maybe accidentally, maybe on purpose. Our grandfather scolds her and becomes so agitated he has a heart attack and dies. He drops dead on the living room floor. My mother moves from room to room, unable to calm herself or take action. She is so confused she unzips her dress. My mother and grandmother are crying and speaking Yiddish in hysterical blasts while my grandfather lies dead on the floor.)

I remember my grandmother as a plump woman with thin hair who cooked large amounts of food that suffused the hallways of her Brooklyn building. She spoke with a thick accent and wrote English in a child's wavy scrawl. All the members of her family and of my grandfather's family were killed during the Holocaust. My mother's first language was Yiddish, although she was born in the United States. She didn't learn English until she went to school.

I ask my mother what my grandmother looked like when she was young, and Toby says, "She was gorgeous. I don't know what happened to the pictures. Maybe Ellen has them." The Pesha I knew looked like a Tartar, and maybe there is Tartar blood in us from Cossacks sweeping down from the Steppes of central Asia. Pesha could have been a cousin of Nureyev's with her jutting cheekbones, hairless, tawny skin, and deep-set eyes that darted mischievously, even in old age. My mother's sister told her their mother had been a sexual adventurer before she married. My mother did not believe this, but Pesha could have been with her looks.

I look at my mother. She seldom meets people's eyes, gazing past them into the middle distance or off to the side, and her shyness surprises me each time I see it. She has been beautiful most of her life, but now there are wrinkles and creases around her eyes. Flesh hangs, wattlelike, under her chin. She still starves herself most of the day, but her middle is thick, and she has lost inches from her height. Her back is straight and no hump is imminent, but several fingers on both hands are crooked from arthritis, which hurts her.

She pops a piece of cookie in her mouth and says, "Wizard number one wouldn't talk to me." She is referring to an eye doctor she consulted about her failing sight. "Even a dog you talk to. He spoke into a tape recorder and sent the notes to Postley. Postley sent me to wizard number two. Everyone told me to wait, but it was taking so long I walked down the hall and marched into his office and said, 'Are you God? It's so hard to see you?' I said, 'Am I going to go blind?'" She sips her tea and looks up. "I have the wet kind of macular degeneration. The dry kind they can treat. Maybe I won't go blind completely, but the doctor said, 'Read as much as you can, now,' so you know what that has to mean."

I ask her to describe a poster of Paris hanging on a wall. She makes out the details and reads the lettering. After we leave the Guggenheim, we walk down Madison Avenue. The streets are thronged with kids arriving home from school, and I remember dashing into the house and calling out, "Ma, I'm home," wanting to see her before grabbing my bike and taking off again. Women with velvet headbands are walking dogs. Toby places her hand gingerly on the head of a cocker spaniel and says, "I'm afraid of dogs. That's how I was raised." The owner says, "You don't seem afraid." My mother says, "I'm afraid of everything. You have no idea."

After she dies, I see her inside a chicken instead of a gizzard, a heart, and a liver. She used to chop chicken in a wooden bowl, throw in green pepper, and lace it with mayonnaise from the health food store. And she would say on more than one occasion but not often, "Have it," and I can tell you it was tasty. I slip slivers of garlic into chicken flesh I stab, opening little mouths and the memory of the knife when my mother's chest was slit and wouldn't heal, and she pointed to the stitched red gash with a cockeyed grin and said, "Like a chicken." "Like a chicken," I said.

IN THE DAYS FOLLOWING MY MOTHER'S BYPASS surgery, there are bruises on her arms from an IV. She has a large, bandaged wound in the middle of her chest and incisions on her legs where veins have been removed for her heart. Her limbs are slack, and her skin is a paper bag. One of her nostrils is larger than the other, and it quivers around the cannula supplying oxygen. Several of her toes are bent in different directions, as if they cannot decide which way to go. A corn on one toe is hard and deep, as if it has logged all the miles she has walked.

One day when I enter her room, she is sitting up, holding a bowl of sliced bananas. She can hold a spoon with her good hand, but she cannot understand why her other hand won't steady the bowl. She looks at one hand, then the other, her brow creased in concentration. She could pick up pieces of banana and place them in her mouth, one at a time, but she picks up the bowl and tosses the contents at her face, catching whatever she can with her tongue, chewing fast and scowling at anyone who tries to remove the fallen pieces from her pillow and chest. When she improves, Ellen and I tell her the story of the banana, and she laughs and asks us to tell it again.

A lung specialist counsels Ellen and me against sending her to a rehab facility, predicting she will die in weeks or at most months. We ignore him and place Toby at the Helen Hayes rehab hospital. Before the transfer is assured, Toby asks again and again, "Will they think I'm worth saving?"

One day in the hospital, a social worker enters Toby's room with a clipboard; Toby needs to decide if she wants to be resuscitated in the event of another heart attack. My mother says to the social worker, "I don't want to be alive, now." The woman pats Toby's shoulder and says, "Give it some thought."

My mother asks what I would do, and I say, "I would want to live." She says, "Why? What's so great about living?" I say, "The story." She waves me away and says, "I don't care about the story. I was never interested in the story." She pauses and looks up. "What is the story?" I say, "Well, history, for one."

She says, "History is a subject I happen to like. History, I have studied, and believe me I have seen things." She looks at her bruised hands. "Maybe I have seen enough." She grips the railing of her bed and says, "People tell you, you are supposed to live for others, but who believes that? Don't misunderstand me. I'm happy to see my children, my grandchildren. I'm happy they're all right. But that is not a reason to live." I say, "You are right. You will have to find other reasons to live." She thinks about this for a moment and tries to hitch herself higher on her pillows. She is collapsing into her weak side, twisting around. I help her adjust. I bring another pillow from the closet and arrange her weak arm so it is comfortable. She says, "Do you remember when you were in high school, and I typed an essay for you, and when we pulled the paper out of the roller we saw it was stuck with bits of chicken?" I say, "Yes." She says, "I wonder how the chicken got there?" I say, "That is the story."

After Toby completes three weeks of acute rehab at Helen Hayes, she transfers from the facility in Nyack to the Hebrew Home in Westchester for additional training. One morning before I visit her, I dream I have a beard. At first only a few black hairs sprout under my chin, but as I look in the mirror hair carpets my face from sideburns to collarbone. It is terrifying, and I laugh.

When I arrive at the Hebrew Home, my mother is in the hall, resting between laps with her physical therapist. She waves to me and sits up taller in her workout suit and sneakers. She is at camp. I am the mother. She is pushing a half walker with her good hand while the therapist supports her on the other side. The therapist says, "Head up, walker forward, right foot forward, weight on your right foot, that's it, you're doing it, bottom in, head up, that's right, now the

left foot. Lift. I've got you, you won't fall, you can do it."
She can.

After her session, I wheel her outside to the patio, and we sit under a tree. Towering oaks shade the lawn, and geese, hunting for food, venture up from the rushing Hudson. I say, "Remember the movie *The Night of the Iguana* when Deborah Kerr wheels her grandfather out and he recites a poem he's been working on for a year?" Toby says, "I'm the grandfather." I say, "He's like an ancient sea turtle, depositing his last egg." She says, "How can a male turtle lay an egg?" I say, "How can you be sitting here with leaves in your hair?"

She says, "I need a dye job." I say she can get her hair done in the home's beauty salon. The place is posh, like a resort. She says, "Deborah Kerr used to play these spinster types who were hot under the hood. That's the way they show the English, refined on the outside but sexed up inside." She looks at her thin arm and says, "I was never hot under the hood." I say, "You were beautiful." She says, "That's what people tell me, but you don't think that about yourself, and besides, that's different from sex. I was afraid of sex."

She points to a woman in a wheelchair and says, "Did you ever see anyone so fat?" The woman fills the seat, and her legs are sausages. Toby says, "How can a person live like that?" I say, "Maybe she is loved for her imperfections." The woman is surrounded by family. Near her, two little girls chase geese. My mother says, "Every misshapen person you defend." I say, "This morning I woke up with a beard." My mother says, "I never wanted children, not if anyone had asked me, which they didn't. I wanted to be a WAC. I thought I would look good in the uniforms."

She says, "Move my arm." I shift her weak hand on the pillow. Her fingers are gnarled. A goose waltzes past, and she tries to pet it with her good hand. The goose scoots away. She says, "What did the poet say in the movie?" I say, "He gave a summation. He was nearly a hundred." The goose sashays up to my mother and looks at her. Toby says, "He wants something. They all want something." Her spine is twisting, and I straighten her. A vein pulses on her neck. Another goose seems on a collision course with her chair. It flaps its wings, and she looks happy until it veers in the direction of the fat woman. Toby looks up and says, "I won't be laying any turtle eggs, if that's what you're expecting. If that's what you're waiting for, you might as well load up the wagons and hitch up the horses."

IN THE 1970S, MY SISTER'S HUSBAND BUYS A HEALTH food store on Fifty-Second Street, and my parents work there, my mother in the front, the czarina of vitamins, my father, the ex–coat manufacturer, in the back, whipping up smoothies and lunch specials. The first thing people ask when they enter is, "Where's Toby?" She is never happier. The shop is the streets. She kibitzes with Greta Garbo, pretending not to know who she is. Greta says, "You, Toby, you know what it is, a man?" My mother shoots a look at Murray, who is slicing an avocado, and says, "That's what I know, end of story."

The store booms for six years until the landlord hikes the rent and my sister's husband is forced to sell. My father dies. My mother becomes a volunteer at God's Love We Deliver, cooking for homebound people with AIDS. Three times a week she stands for three-hour shifts, dicing onions, potatoes, and carrots. She is part of a crowd, and her friends drag her out for coffee and Chinese food. God's Love is what she talks about: Karen's dating debacles, Ben's heart murmur. I volunteer there, too, and one day the head chef calls me and says Toby is making racist remarks. They have put up with it for more than a year. He asks me to speak to her.

I go to her apartment, and we sit at the cherrywood table with the walnut, harlequin inlays. She says, "May I be struck down by lightning if I ever said such a thing." She doesn't look me in the eye. She says, "They're lying."

I say, "Frankie says you talk about *them*. You use the word *shvartses*. Everyone knows what that means."

Toby shakes her head and presses her lips together and says, "You're siding with strangers? I should have known. You'd sell me down the river so people will like you. You'd stab me in the back."

"I'm on your side," I say, but how can this be true? She wants my allegiance no matter what. I want hers. We want what we want.

She faces a plaque on the wall, a reproduction from the Met depicting a lion crouching at the feet of galloping horses. The lion is mighty in himself with eyes ablaze, but he's cornered. Toby says, "Who the hell are they to tell me what I can and cannot say? What, I'm going to be fired from a volunteer job?"

I say, "How would you feel if people slammed Jews?" She says, "They hate Jews! That's why they're ganging up on me." I say, "Ma, you're doing the same thing." She says, "People are jealous of Jews. Blacks deserve what they get." I say, "*All* black people?" She says, "No. Some, I like."

I say, "Well, you have to think about other people's feelings." She sets down her cup, and the saucer rattles. She says, "I don't want to be gagged."

I say, "Just stop being nasty. How hard is that?" This is a question I ask myself every day. Mornings I wake up with lists of friends I've offended. The rats that survive are the ones that adapt. The rats with the happiest memories survive the longest.

Toby is silent for a moment, searching for a way to be herself and remain at the party. In the end, she is asked to leave. When she reports this, she looks sad and ashamed, and I feel for her, but then color flushes her cheeks, and she says, "I don't need them. I don't need to work there anymore."

DURING HER LAST MONTHS, SHE GOES IN AND OUT of dementia. When her aides go shopping, she flings herself from her wheelchair to the floor and tumbles to the door, bringing down tables and chairs. She can't walk, but there is strength in her right hand and leg. She strips off her clothes, crawls naked into the hall, and bangs on the doors of her neighbors. Other times she wheels herself to the elevator, rides to the lobby, and tells the doormen her aides are abusing her. She wants contact. Every time she falls, she has to be picked up and held. Before her stroke, she was reluctant to be touched. Afterward, she kisses the hands of strangers and slides them across her cheeks. She is scared that Primrose, who has been with her since she left rehab, will storm away. I say, "She won't."

My sister tells a story. My mother is having coffee after a class at Hunter College when a voice burns through the cafeteria din. It is my mother's sister, Bell, and she says to Toby with a bitter rasp, "So, you're still alive." Bell disappears like an apparition, or maybe Toby lowers her head or flees. According to Toby, a week later a card arrives in the mail with a picture of a snake on it, signed Bell. I say to Ellen, "Do you believe this happened?" My mother's address and phone number are not listed.

One afternoon as my mother nears death, Ellen calls her and Primrose asks her if she knows who Ellen is. Toby says, "My sister." I think Toby may be confusing the name *Ellen* with the name *Bell*, or mixing up the words *daughter* and *sister*. Soon after this call, when Ellen visits Toby, Toby recalls a quarrel with Bell, and Ellen says, "She's probably dead." Toby bursts into tears, saying she has seen Bell on TV: "She was waving to me."

On the phone, my mother says, "Primrose says you come to New York every week and don't visit me." I say, "It's not true." She says, "That's what Primrose says." Toby reminds me of my grandmother when she was old and confused. She once called me to report she had read Toby's obituary in a newspaper and wanted to know where her daughter was buried. I said Toby was alive and well, wondering if my grandmother preferred a daughter who was dead to a daughter who had shut her out of her life.

On the phone, Toby asks if I have children. I say, "No." She says, "Why not?" I say, "They're not that easy to produce." She says, "I thought you would have six by now." I look at my hands that are my mother's hands, small boned and veiny. I miss her as if she were already dead.

IT IS 2007, AND I AM PUSHING MY MOTHER'S WHEELCHAIR up the hill on Fifty-Seventh Street. Primrose walks beside her. Toby is nearing ninety-two.

My mother says, "Toothpaste, cotton swabs, witch hazel." Her fists are waving. She is bundled in a wool coat and a fake fur hat that frames her pretty, hollowed face. Primrose says, "You told me twenty times." Her jaw is clenched, her eyebrows are to the roof. Primrose is what separates my mother from a nursing home. She is wearing a navy parka and a wool hat pulled low over red dreadlock extensions. My mother absently holds a glove, and Primrose pockets it.

I ask my mother if she is happy to be out, and she says in a reedy voice, "How can I be happy?" It is a question she might have asked at any stage of her life. I see more strain than usual beneath the dimples that etch her cheeks—a smeared, blitzed look, like one of those murdered or murderous faces painted by Francis Bacon.

As we wait for a light on Columbus Circle, Toby says, "Don't give up your apartment. Don't be stupid." Cars whiz close to the curb. The glass-clad Time Warner Center, New York City's first enclosed shopping mall—with chic restaurants and boutiques—rises impassively over the empty fountain surrounding a statue of the Italian mariner. It's as if he has come all this way to be at the party, the New York everyone feels shipwrecked from if they have to leave. Two mounted police patrol the gate of the park. Vendors sell souvenirs and framed photographs, including the famous shot of John Lennon, with his round specs and shoulder-length mane, perched on a ledge on the Upper West Side. If Richard and I can return here, my place can be a base, although it's too small to live in for long, and jobs in museum studies are rare. It is a law of the universe—as fixed as the principle that mass and energy are interchangeable—you don't abandon a rent-stabilized apartment in New York. You maintain your resident status, holding a chair and a whip against landlords.

Yet I seem not to care. I am floating, balloonlike, over my life: my early childhood in Washington Heights, my student days at Columbia, my tenure at the *Village Voice*, my loves and friends, all tangled in the spaghetti streets of New York. It is so much my element I can't feel it. Does a fish know it's swimming in water?

At Columbus Circle, it doesn't occur to me that my mother fears leaving *her* apartment. She fears her aides will scatter, worn-out by her demands, and she will be exiled from the only existence that breathes life into her and that she sharpens with her huffing theatrics, my mother the character, my mother with a role in the only show she wants to attend. Even in her wheelchair, she rides buses to Fairway, searching for a nectarine that won't break her heart. I say her aides won't leave, but it makes no dent. I don't consider she is worried about me. I can't hear her. I can't hear my friends who say, "Don't lose your bearings. Don't lose yourself." I think they are saying, "You can't have love. You can't have happiness." They say, "Look before you leap," but the landscape looks like Richard.

Primrose says, "Laurie is not giving up her apartment." To me she says, "I tell her this ten times a day."

The sky is gray and pillowy. A light rain falls. A police horse comes close, the smell of its wet hair filling the air. The horse snorts, and my mother flinches back and says, "I'm afraid of horses. Please, Laurie, don't let the horse get so close. It will step on me. It will bite me." Prim says, "More likely you'll bite the horse." She is eyeing Toby with the affection of their early days, her mouth swerving to the side. She has played reggae for Toby and danced, my mother exclaiming how talented she is, how sexy. They talk about sex, Prim lying beside Toby on her bed. Toby has learned the Jamaican words for sex parts—*punaani, cockie,* and *batty hole*—and she likes to say them. For a moment, Prim is Island Girl again, her hips swaying and her laugh full throated, the beauty from St. Ann's and later Kingston who walked through fields of ginger and annatto, a gorgeous woman pursued by men, who married one, only to cut him loose when he proved more an

My Life as an Animal

anchor than a float. She has made me swear not to tell Toby about a new man she is seeing. She doesn't want to hear my mother tear him down.

Toby says, "Me bite a horse? I don't even like horses." Prim says, "You don't like anything. You don't need anything, do you, Toby?" My mother presses her lips together. "That's right. I wish I could live alone."

The light changes, and we cross. A pack of teenagers with a rainbow of skin colors lope past us. Behind them an elderly couple navigate without assistance. My mother glares at them enviously. Two Wall Street types in long coats and leather boots bound up from the subway, jog to make the light, and disappear into the Time Warner Center. A bus wheezes to a halt and coughs out sundry denizens, some heading for shops, others for Eighth Avenue. When we reach the other side of the street, I press down on the handlebars of my mother's chair, and she swings back like a patient at the dentist's.

She says, "Why are you going to Arizona?" I say, "To be with Richard." I hoist her up to the curb. She says, "Do you pay for your plane tickets?" I say, "Yes." She says, "Why?" I say, "I want to be with Richard." She says, "I wish I had your money." She chuckles and twists her head around and says, "Why are you giving up your apartment?" I say, "I'm not." She says, "You said you were giving up your apartment." I say, "I didn't." She says, "You don't know how things will turn out. Where will you go? Don't be a fool. No one gives up an apartment in New York. Why doesn't he come to you?" I say, "He has a job."

She turns her face to the side as we make our way through the glass doors, and I wheel her across the marble rotunda. Her profile is still beautiful. Her cheekbones jut out glamorously. She says, "He's a poor slob," speaking in a dreamy, mad hatter voice, addressing the air more than me. "Poor slob," she says again and again.

EIGHT MONTHS BEFORE MY MOTHER DIES, SHE IS admitted to St. Luke's Hospital after a psychiatrist deems her in crisis. The aim is to start her on a new mood stabilizer, the previous ones having failed. My sister is fed up with my mother, who is screaming pretty much all the time. But Toby touches me and reminds me of Al Swearengen, the sympathetic monster at the center of the TV series *Deadwood*, who also reminds me of myself. Played by British actor Ian Mc-Shane, his dark eyes ringed with pain, Al steels himself for the next brutality he is about to unleash on the world, as if his savagery is against his will, as if his cruelty is a tyrant driving the obliging but reluctant servant who is also him.

I call Toby on her ninety-second birthday. She says, "I disappointed you by not giving you money and by calling Richard a poor slob." I say, "Why did you say that?" She says, "I didn't mean anything. I say the same things about Mark." Mark is my sister's husband. I say, "You've known Mark for forty years. You've never even met Richard." She says, "You're right."

It seems she is seeing herself more clearly as she slips away. Primrose has been coaching her. She doesn't know if Primrose is right, but she loves her friend. My mother says, "I'm sorry," but she does not give me the money.

SEVEN WEEKS BEFORE SHE DIES, SHE IS ADMITTED TO the hospital with mysterious bleeding. Doctors suspect bladder cancer, but I do not believe she has cancer. I think she will return to her apartment and I will see her again. She will meet Richard, even if she has no idea who we are. It turns out

66   *My Life as an Animal*

she does not have cancer. She dies in her bed, approaching ninety-three.

On the phone, driving to Toby's apartment, Ellen says, "She's gone." She is calm. She sounds numb. After my mother's stroke, we learned she had fibrosis of the lung, which is incurable and untreatable. It was supposed to have killed her a long time ago, and finally it has. According to the coroner, Toby suffocated in her own fluids.

Richard speaks about two types of museums. One, like Noah's Ark, aims to exhibit samples of everything that exists. An example is the American Museum of Natural History in New York. The second kind are memory palaces, housing idiosyncratic collections or commemorating local history. You find them in any small town.

I sleep in Toby's bed. I organize her things, and we learn her furniture is valuable. A lamp, for instance, is the work of the Italian designer Gino Sarfatti. I vote to auction it all, including a small table I have thought of keeping. Toby wore a deco diamond ring on her left pinky, and I would follow it as her hand swept this way and that. She used to say, "You will have it when I'm dead," and she would smile, unable to imagine her extinction, same as everybody. On my last visit to her in the hospital, I didn't understand why she was wearing the ring. I thought it might be a comfort to her, so I did not remove it for safekeeping. When it was stolen, I felt the ground move out from under me, and I felt I was falling. I am falling now.

I make my way through Toby's freezer, cooking pieces of chicken, bent like her fingers. I pack up a set of gleaming black plates with silver trim, service for twelve, never used. Outside, my mother still skitters along Fifty-Eighth Street. She stands in front of the Plaza Hotel on the red carpet, secured with brass rivets, chatting with the doorman while scanning the distance for the dot that is me. If I am a minute late, she fears I have been abducted by aliens. I should be so lucky.

Toby would not have cared about the garbage bags stuffed with her clothes, still in plastic from the cleaner's, and her chipped, everyday plates with the autumn-leaf design worn faint. I throw away a dozen pairs of Easy Spirit shoes, "character-style," with a strap across the instep. I see my mother folded over a book, a conservative talk show blasting on the radio. When she is assigned the works of an author in one of her classes, she reads the writer's entire oeuvre. She is reading at the dining table, above her glows the modernist chandelier with its burst of tulip fixtures. In the late 1950s, when our bungalow in Long Beach was converted into an all-year-round house, my mother trotted behind the decorator, Julie Stein, as he decided how we would live.

AT THE START OF A HIKE, I STAND ON THE ROAD WHILE Richard studies trails. He explains where we are going, but I don't care. I know the walk will be arduous and hot and I will not exactly enjoy it. I will want to go along, hoping to see lizards and birds. Hikers share trails with mountain bikers. What they do—bobbling up crazily steep paths and hurtling down the other side—looks torturous, but it is the ordeal you choose, a dare that feels like a right to exist.

Shade is beautiful in the desert, cutting a knife-edge against glaring light, bleeding across wide, vacant space. One day Richard and I arrive at the top of a hill, and he sees a still higher point crowned by black, jutting rocks. As we scurry up, we realize we have come to the old wall of a fortified area. A small sign indicates an archaeological site, but it isn't marked

My Life as an Animal

to attract visitors. Around us are hundreds of petroglyphs: designs scraped out on black desert varnish by people who lived in the region nine hundred years ago. All traces of their culture have vanished except for these tags, and no one knows what they mean. Some guess they are astronomical and astrological symbols, or directional pointers, or territorial markers, or personal and artistic expressions. I copy a design into my notebook, a pared-down, twig thing, a remnant of ourselves we carry inside.

When I think about New York, I see my mother's feet stretching down to the Lower East Side, her hands up to Carnegie Hall. I have pictures of my parents when they were young and sleek, their hair thick and wavy. Sometimes they're posed on horseback and skis—sports they did not know how to do. The country settings make them look all the more urban.

My mother dreams she is running for a bus. A man with a mustache guides her up the steps, and she says, "I'm not young anymore. I wish I had your youth, darling, I wish you good health, you are so kind." I see her on her bed, pulled behind a boat. She is flying across waves and she is afraid, but that is the element she remembers as her music. Even as a girl, her eyebrows knitted together as if seeking each other in consolation. We don't know who we are. It isn't a human capacity, so you might as well wish for a golden beak to sprout from the parrot-colored feathers on your face. "I'm sorry for your loss," people say, but what is my loss? I am glad we will not meet again. I wish she were alive.

GESCHE

On a train to Berlin, I met a doctor, Gesche, who was beautiful in a worn-out way from late nights at hospitals. She was stylish, with long legs and hair extensions piled high, and her skin was tan and looked very dark against the gleaming white shirt and gold necklace she wore. It was a long journey, and we got to talking.

She was a neurosurgeon who had switched to pediatric oncology, having grown weary of the condescension of men in her field. She had grown tired, too, of the anonymity of her patients, most of whom arrived at the hospital with head traumas from car accidents. She would operate, change a dressing, and never see the person again. She moved to Canada, entered oncology, and began treating children. Some of her patients remained in her care for years, and as the German countryside rolled along with its neat villages and puffy clouds, she recalled a visit to the grave of a young girl she had thought she could save. The girl's mother was pregnant again, and she and Gesche had cried in each other's arms. Gesche paled at the memory, and I wondered where the blood had gone.

I knew in a way, but I liked thinking about the body in the company of a scientist. When I was twenty-seven, I considered applying to medical school in order to give my life purpose. Then I thought about what doctors actually spend their time doing.

In Canada, Gesche fell in love with a cell biologist who was studying aging. She said, "All that cells want—whether healthy cells or tumor cells—is more." She was evoking an erotics of aliveness. She was suggesting that existence feels like desire, even on a cellular level and even when we are in pain. This idea appealed to me. I thought it meant things were not our fault. She described sex with the cell biologist as if we were not strangers, and I felt we were not. We were part of a band of restless women who find each other on trains and in lobbies. I was falling in love with her the way I fall in love with people I don't know.

One morning in Berlin, we met for breakfast. Gesche had worked all night, caring for premature babies—a rotation required for practicing in Germany again. Some of the babies had spent only twenty-five weeks in the womb. She put out her hand, as if holding a pound of butter, to show me how small they were. Their brains were not developed enough to regulate swallowing and breathing. She had to take blood from veins too tiny to see. I worried these technologies could make it harder for women to choose abortions, and I feared for the development of the small beings. I asked how it felt to do this work. She threw back her head and stretched out her arms. She was wearing a long sweater and skinny black pants. Her eyebrows were fuzzy and dark, and her dimples were deep. She said, "I feel competent. It's thrilling."

She asked about being a writer, and I described the scene in *Stardust Memories* when a space alien says to the Woody

Allen character, "You want to do a service for mankind? Tell funnier jokes." She smiled. I did not know if she could imagine a life of sitting alone in a room. She ordered eggs, a baguette, and coffee, and we talked under an umbrella as yellow jackets buzzed the jam. She was thirty-six, and life billowed out before her. She had the work she wanted, and she had love.

She and the cell biologist were considering having a child, but she had doubts. She said, "We don't share a common language." She did not mean German or English. She meant what was big to her was small to him, and vice versa. I remembered the steps I had taken leading up to having a child and the steps I had taken leading away from the decision. They were not steps. I had decided nothing.

The cell biologist was older than Gesche and set in his ways. She said, "He thinks he knows what a man is and what a woman is, and he thinks he has science on his side." She rolled her eyes. A bee got caught in honey. It extracted one foot, believing it was free, and then another foot got stuck. She took my hand, and I saw green flecks in her eyes. She smiled uncertainly and said, "I don't take what men say seriously. Men are not their words."

I thought, If we are not our words, what are we? Then I wondered what we might be apart from words. Gesche was reaching for the everything that does not exist, and I thought, Don't do it. Don't give yourself away. Then I thought, Why not?

BOULDER

Richard and I are in a café in the outskirts of London, on a visit to one of his sisters. He says, "They hate us," meaning the waiters. He thinks it is too near closing and we should leave. I say, "They don't hate us." The café is open for another forty-five minutes, and I have ordered tea. He says, "You don't pick up social cues." I go back to writing in my notebook, and his eyes bore into the top of my head. I can feel them swiveling around on bony projections, like the eyes of a crab.

The café is in a building made of glass. A band of Nordics with blond ponytails and khaki knapsacks carry their cups to the trash. Richard jabs my elbow and says, "See?"

I once had a boyfriend who was always looking at his watch. We were not together long enough for me to get sick of him. I was like a dog you hold out a stick to, and the dog keeps biting the end of the stick. Another boyfriend once said, "The power in a relationship resides in the person who is willing to leave." He was the person willing to leave.

Richard and I have spent the day at Kew Gardens—a remnant of the Victorian ambition to collect samples of everything. In this case, botanical specimens. We walked a course atop fifty-foot trees, where a plaque reports that England is home to nine million trees. How do they know? We saw the oldest potted plant in existence, *Encephalartos altensteinii*, a Jurassic cycad—a species that predates flowering plants and once shaded dinosaurs as they lumbered around the planet. This plant was over three hundred years old, and it was easy to see how it had survived: it lived in its own pot.

I start to worry about our plants in Arizona. Then I remember our friend Bill kept them alive the summer before. I switch to worrying about my plants in New York. My friend Adam is looking after them and has already killed a pot of pansies. I don't mention this to Richard. He would say, "You don't have to voice every thought that comes into your head. Most people don't say most of what they think." I would say, "They don't?" He would say, "No."

In the café I write about David Nash, whose sculptures are installed around the grounds and galleries of Kew. Nash uses dead trees, hedges, twigs, sod, and seeds in his work, and I become aware I am more interested in art made of natural materials than in nature itself, even the woven carpet of a garden. When I look at nature, I disappear. It is relaxing, but only up to a point. At the center of Nash's show is a series of sculptures carved from a giant tree that died on a mountain in Wales. The tree's life is over, but wood goes on seeming alive. The growth rings look like the scales of fish and the cells of a beehive. The tree is a body with arms, legs, a trunk, and bones—its scars and fractures intact. And in this body Nash has found boats, benches, boxes, and a rough pig with twig legs.

The most powerful piece is a film Nash shot about a boulder he carved in 1978, when the tree was discovered. After he finished carving the boulder, it proved so heavy he decided to float it down the mountain along a cascading stream. He filmed the process, and he kept filming, because nothing he envisioned came to pass. Early in the boulder's journey, it became snagged on rocks. After a year or so, it hurtled to another perch where it was trapped again, and after several years of watching the boulder buried in snow and darkened by iron in the rushing stream, after watching it erode and become etched with ridges that took on the features of a forbearing face, after seeing the boulder bob like a seal and float into a salt marsh and sit stranded on a plain of mud like the last speaker of its language, Nash decided it belonged to the mountain and sea, and he did not try to move it to his studio. The film documents the boulder's history until 2003, when Nash saw it for the last time. Other people sighted it in 2008, but it has not been seen since.

Richard and I sat on backless leather benches, and as images of the boulder and the stream rushed by, I felt swept along on the journey. On the wall beside us was a text written by Nash that took my breath away: "The boulder is not lost. It is wherever it is."

In the café, a man who looks South Asian and speaks with a British accent prepares our tea. Everywhere in England, we float on waves of multiculturalism, immigration, and legacies of empire. It is easy to think you are in a place where everyone is a traveler and therefore everyone can find a niche, although no one is home.

Richard left England half a lifetime ago. He keeps saying, "England doesn't feel like home anymore." Both his parents have recently died, and he no longer knows the slang. He means he is in mourning. He means he does not see a way back.

He gestures to the man behind the counter and says, "He wants us to leave." I close my notebook. Richard says, "I wish

I weren't like this." His eyes slide to the edge of the table. He says, "Thanks for accepting me." I snort. The day before we had agreed to wander around London and get lost. As soon as we set off he opened a map and suggested routes we could walk, as if we had a destination. Wherever we were, he charted our way back to Bloomsbury, as if never leaving was the goal. After a while, he put the map away. I said, "You can look at it if you want to." He said, "This is more fun." I knew it was not fun for him, but later in a café he wrote, "Location is all about arrival, although arrival might not exist."

Another day he said, "I am the most patient person you know." I believed him, and then I wondered if this was an example of mind control. I tried to think of other people who liked me more than Richard, and no one surfaced. I tried to think of someone I liked more than him and drew a blank.

After we leave Kew, we comb Bloomsbury for a place to eat. As we stroll, we pass a man in a wheelchair, and Richard says, "There will come a time when we won't be able to walk as much as now." He laughs and says, "What should I do with you when you die?" I say, "Burn my body and toss the ashes in a bin." He says, "What, no service? No gathering at the apartment for a glass of sherry and fond remembrances?" I say, "No one will care as much as you."

That night in a tapas bar, I write about Richard and me at the café. He writes about the boulder, pointing out that Nash changed his art project. Instead of showing the boulder in a gallery, he presented a collaboration with the natural environment. I say, "That's really interesting." Richard says, "With this kind of art, you look less at the object and more at what it makes you feel. The boulder asks us to think about how we measure success. It asks us to think about what is given and what can change."

He sips his wine and dips a bread stick in olive oil. A light comes into his eyes. He says, "The story of the boulder and the story of us in the café are versions of each other. That's why the movie went into us. Sometimes the boulder is a rock, sometimes it's wood, sometimes it's an animal. It gets stuck, and so do we. Both of us are the boulder, and both of us are the water, swirling around. We are big and weighty to each other, but a relationship changes as it gets rubbed."

I say, "I could never have come up with that in a million years." He says, "Yes, you could have."

LEAVING GARDNER

In the fall of 2009, I was staying in an apartment near where my old friend Evelyn lived, and I hoped I would run into her. It had been a couple of years. Sometimes we showed up at the same feminist event. She would say my name, her voice rising as if seeing a ghost. I would be happy to see her, always happy to see her Russian cheekbones and creamy skin.

I called our mutual friend Albert, who said, "Call her if you like, but I don't think it's going to do you any good." He sighed. "My dear, you have faded from her thoughts."

Still, as I crossed Washington Square Park, I wondered if her number was in my phone. It was blustery out, and the paths were plastered with yellow ginkgo leaves and fallen nuts that smelled like dirty socks. Girls in tights and short skirts and boys with stubbly faces and baggy pants were rushing to classes at NYU. Evelyn used to say I was brave. She meant I surrendered easily. I didn't have her number, but a combination came into my head. I called it, and there was her voice on a machine. I said I was in New York and asked if she would like to meet.

When I think about Evelyn, I think about Gardner. In 1990, when Gardner was dying in the hospital, I was with

Evelyn in a coffee shop. We sat at a Formica table with silver squiggles in the surface. I was forty-four, and Evelyn was fifty-six, and her voice had taken on a sandpapery rasp, as if experience tasted bitter, like broccoli rabe. She propped her elbows on the table and narrowed her eyes. A little smile lifted the corners of her mouth. She said, "You will have a chance now to loosen your grip on men."

GARDNER AND I WERE WALKING UP BROADWAY, AND he was dragging. I said, "Can you pick up the pace?" At a light, he said, "I've been tired." He looked at the traffic for a place to dump his fear. "I jogged around the block, and it felt like I'd run five miles. I walked up a flight of stairs, and my legs felt like lead." He waved his hand and said, "It must be a postviral thing. Remember a few weeks ago when I felt low? It must have been flu." I did not remember any flu, and viruses didn't quit and come back. Or maybe they did. Was he thinner? Why was he so slow?

The next week he learned he had bone marrow cancer. It was June, 1990, and he would be dead six months later. Albert was in the room when Gardner learned the diagnosis. I arrived a few minutes later, and Gardner handed me a card with the name of his doctor. He said, "She will explain things." His chest rose and fell slowly under a thin sheet.

After he was transfused, we walked the hospital corridors, glimpsing terminal patients through open doors. Their skin was yellow. They lay in fetal coils like the stunned victims of Pompeii. I looked at Gardner's muscles, still firm.

One afternoon while he was in the hospital, I sat by a fountain that muted wheezing buses and shrieking horns, and I became aware of other solitaries, reading or looking out. I was reading *London Fields*, by Martin Amis, and I came to a passage where the narrator observes that masturbation is almost never described in fiction. Solitary pleasure, it struck me, is seldom portrayed in literature. Aloneness is something we are supposed to be spared if we live right. Aloneness is a referendum on our fitness for love. Don't we all believe that a little?

Gardner wanted to understand his illness but only up to a point. Details dissolved in his head. Twenty years ago the average survival rate for bone marrow cancer was three years, but I did not know that at first and Gardner did not ask how long he had. He knew he would die sooner than he had hoped, but his body had not let him down before, and he had already cheated death. During World War II he had flown reconnaissance missions, a thousand miles out from Tinian to Japan, a thousand miles back on a single tank of gas, nothing below but roiling waves. Forty percent of his unit were shot down or crash-landed on carriers. One morning Gardner had a stomachache and stayed back. That plane disappeared. He was twenty-one. When we were first together he would not swim in the ocean. He said, "I have seen enough water."

We met at a tennis court in East Hampton in 1976. He was fifty-six and married to a woman named Frances. Their marriage was up and down. I was thirty and living with a man named Robert. Robert and I were hitting the ball with Gardner's sons, and a man with silver hair, blue eyes, and ruddy skin watched through the fence. Sex and melancholy rose off him. Two years passed. One day I said I was going to the city, and Gardner said he would be there, too. We had dinner. I was supposed to meet a friend, but I did not get out of the car.

At this time, he was sleeping with a woman in her forties and another woman in her thirties. He said his marriage to Frances was dead. It may have been dead, but it wasn't buried. Friday nights, he would return to their house in East Hampton. Sunday nights he would drive back to New York. I would hear his footsteps in the hall and leap up. The door would open, and we would stand in the living room, our clothes falling off like leaves.

In the hospital, Gardner's roommate was named Piero, a wealthy Tuscan who spoke with a musical accent, an interior designer, a gay man who addressed Gardner in a coy, chiding tone as if teasing a boy, as if Gardner had a full life ahead. They sat in armchairs in striped robes, munching dried figs and looking out at the sea: Piero at the Lido in Rome, Gardner at Montauk.

Piero was dying of lymphoma. The cancer had progressed to his brain, and his skin was the color of butter. More than anything, he wanted to return to his apartment and live out his days under the care of a nurse. His vision was failing, and he feared he would not be able to read. He had no family in New York, although friends phoned. In the months ahead, Gardner would return to the hospital many times to see Piero. He would stay connected to Piero when he went in and out of consciousness but could still hear voices if someone spoke directly into his ear. Gardner would say, his blue eyes searching my face, "I could get lymphoma," and I would say, "I don't think you will." His disease did not advance that way.

After he died, I studied his lab reports and interviewed his doctors. Now, more than twenty years later, his death is alive. His paintings and the furniture he designed fill my apartment. Not a day passes when I do not think about him. We fall in love with people we don't pick, not really. Love falls over you like a weather condition, a wolf's paw, a cape.

I WAS THIRTY-TWO WHEN I BECAME FRIENDS WITH EVELYN.
I was established at the *Village Voice*, where she had gotten
her start. She had moved on to writing books, and I wanted
my life to go that way, too. She was lonely, and for a number
of years I was a friend she could rely on. Evelyn, Albert, and
I were a threesome, especially on weekends when Gardner
was in East Hampton. Albert was a gay man who spent more
time with women and straight men than with gay men. The
three of us were active in the women's movement and in gay
liberation. Albert and Evelyn were a couple, and I was their
niece or weird spawn. Evelyn and I were sisters. I did not see
much of Ellen in those years.

In Evelyn's mind, she was every intelligent woman who
had been sold short because she did not come from money
and maybe did not have the best haircut. Basically, she was
Jane Eyre, looking into the hazy hills from Thornfield Hall,
yearning to be recognized as a creature of spirit and mind.
If you asked her what spirit was, she would narrow her eyes
and say, "How can you not know?" In her mind, too, there
was always a fabulous dinner she had not been invited to,
where people with the most mind and spirit carved the world
into understandings. Susan Sontag was at that dinner. Susan
Sontag was not a feminist. She wasn't a feminist because
feminism wasn't a glamorous position. It asked people to ex-
amine their ideas about what a woman is and what a man
is, and some of the people it questioned were drawing up
the guest lists of fabulous parties. In the 1960s and 1970s
the feminists I knew were not looking for a pass through the
door. They were looking to bust up the party.

Evelyn created her own salons, mixing feminists, leftists,
gay activists, theater people, and artists. Her parties would

be noisy and fluid, fifty or sixty bodies crammed into her two rooms, and sex would be ricocheting off the walls, the kind of sex that rises up from excited conversation and the feeling of being in the place where everything you care about is going on. At two in the morning a group would settle in the living room. Someone would introduce a topic, and then, like a jazz improvisation, others would build on the ideas. At three or four, Albert and I would help Evelyn clean up. We were always the last to leave. Her place had to be ordered so she could sit down to work the next day.

Several times a week Evelyn and I walked the city, miles and miles with my dog. We went to movies and plays, hung out at book parties. Weekends we would hike in the hills near a tiny cottage she had built in upstate New York. She understood my attraction to Gardner. She, too, had had a long relationship with an older man—a Communist and a reformer—who was married. She enjoyed Gardner's madcap quality, and she would join us for drinks at the Palace Hotel, where for several years he painted trompe l'oeil designs on the walls.

A friend had introduced Gardner to Leona Helmsley, and she had taken a liking to him and hired him to transform her hotel. The job included a free hotel room on the eighteenth floor along with room service for the first five months of a three-year commission. Those were the heady days of fluffy robes, Gulf shrimp and smoked salmon, a bathtub for two, and sweeping views of the sparkling city. Gardner marbleized columns, sponged clouds onto domes, and applied gold and silver leaf to moldings. He set up a workshop in the attic, a rococo Santa factory, where he cast plaster pineapples and moon faces. Mostly he worked the graveyard shift from midnight to five, when the dining room was closed.

Sometimes I helped him, wheeling scaffolding through the lobby, catching the night rule of hustlers and sharks.

In July 1982, my father died of liver cancer a mere five weeks after learning he was ill. During the month of August, Gardner and I rented a house in East Hampton, where I worked on an article about the right-to-life movement. Directly following my father's funeral, I drove to a right-to-life convention in Cherry Hill, New Jersey, where I inspected a closet of fetuses in bottles. Shelf after shelf, their giant heads pressed against the glass. It was as if a child had gone berserk and drowned all her dolls. The shock value of such props is that we can't detach from the sad pickled beings, and the grotesqueness of all that death, on one side the womb and on the other the grave, was funny in a way I think of as Jewish.

Evelyn was this kind of Jew as well. One spring at an artist colony she became friends with a painter, and when I asked her what the woman looked like, she said, "A monkey." We had a mutual friend in the women's movement whose face I thought had a simian cast. I said, "Like Helena?" Evelyn said, "No, a different kind of monkey."

She came to stay with Gardner and me in East Hampton that August. She wasn't fussy about sleeping arrangements or food, just conversation. In her honor I threw a dinner party and invited as many accomplished people as I could find, but that night she got into a fight about literature or politics, her almond eyes narrowing. She fought in the style of the cafeteria and stoop. "That's not true," she would say before the person could finish a thought. "What are you *talking* about?" she would spit, her mouth twisting. It was like watching myself. On speed.

I stayed out of the fray, slipping from the kitchen, where I chopped things, to the table, where I served pasta and salad.

I knew Evelyn was spoiling the party, but I did not want to blame her. I was worried she wasn't having a good time.

After dessert, we piled into Gardner's station wagon and drove to the beach, but as the moon cast shadows and the surf whipped against the black jetties, Evelyn continued to drive home her points, as if arguing was warming her in the cool mist.

When we got back to the house and people headed for their cars, I saw Sasha was not with us. How was this possible? I went everywhere with the dog. I was the dog. Gardner and I raced back to the beach. I was terrified he had run away or been hurt. I would deserve it. He was in the parking lot, pacing back and forth in the place where he had last smelled us, his eyes glowing in the headlight glare. He had a black terrier face with a white body, a plumy tail, fluffy knickers, and the legs of a goat. He dived at us when he saw us and looked at me as if to say, "What was that?" I said, "Evelyn."

AFTER GARDNER CAME HOME FROM THE HOSPITAL, HE worked on a series of paintings. His abstractions had long been filled with fins and skies, the arcs of aircraft, flickers and flashes of light. His work was marked by a luminous quality, and added to that over the last few years were darker currents. The paintings he now produced, at once grave and rapturous, bristled with new tension as he raced against the clock.

The drugs he was taking did not cause nausea, and at night we walked. One night we crossed Central Park and continued south a couple of miles. I wanted to keep going. I thought death would not catch us if we kept walking. The air was warm under a full moon. Gardner said, "I've walked enough," and we took a cab, and I knew our life would never be the same.

I dreamed we were in a car that would not go in reverse. I got out, and Gardner drove away. I dreamed I moved to a run-down part of a city, and my rooms were exposed to shops and passersby. Strangers wandered in, rude and demanding. The living room floor was as steep as a ski slope, and I wondered how I could keep Gardner's furniture from slipping off. I dreamed Gardner collapsed at my feet and his blood drained out, but when we got to the hospital I was the patient.

At the beginning of August on a warm, clear day, we drove to the Berkshires, where I was on assignment to review plays for the *Voice*. I was at the wheel, and Mozart was on the radio, and I was happy. That's how I remember it. During the drive we ate yogurt, and when we pulled into Stockbridge I saw Gardner had jumbled my expense receipts with the sticky lids. I complained. He didn't apologize. I said he was careless, as if carelessness had caused his cancer. He shouted and threatened to take the bus home. And then there was no one in the world I wanted more.

That night we saw Athol Fugard's play *The Road to Mecca*, about an aging artist who is nearly destroyed by isolation and whose work sustains her. Teresa Wright played the central character, and Gardner and I wept through the performance. Later we slept entwined until, near dawn, there was a thunderous crash. Sasha had tumbled down unfamiliar stairs. He was all right, but when I went back to sleep I dreamed he chewed off his leg and left it on the bed.

In Lenox, I offered to buy Gardner a new bag for his golf clubs. He said no. We found a tennis court and hit for several hours as hawks circled lazily overhead. We roamed the Clark museum in Williamstown, Gardner flipping his glasses on and off to inspect the brushstrokes on the Homers and Sargents. In the months to come, he would say many times, "I am not giving up." He did not accept his death, not even when it was days away.

In mid-August a lump appeared on his wrist. He said he had strained himself opening the trunk of his car. He had twisted the key so hard it had broken in the lock. His oncologist did not want to perform a biopsy because his white count was suppressed and surgery could lead to infection. He said, "I'm not worried, but I think the lump is ugly." I said, "It doesn't look ugly." In September his flesh began to sag. Did he see it? Another lump formed inside his mouth where a tooth had been extracted. This lump was hard.

I said, "Try not to worry." I was boiling water for tea. He circled the kitchen and said, "How can I not worry with a lump on my wrist and now this one in my mouth? It has to be bad." I said, "Cortez said your counts are up." I stirred sugar into his cup. He said, "What does it mean? What does any of it mean?" He left the tea on the counter.

The lump in his mouth was biopsied and revealed cancerous plasma cells. Cortez said the chemo would destroy them, just as it targeted cancer in other parts of his body. She was a beautiful brunette in the style of Demi Moore with fanatical eyes. I would get caught up in her optimism and then, out of her force field, I would think, What is she talking about? A hundred times a day Gardner ran his tongue over the lump.

In October, he had no appetite and looked exhausted and thin. He said, "I have no enthusiasm. I'm not myself." We held each other. We took taxis and buses. His voice grew weak, and he didn't paint. A pulse beat appeared on his chest, as if his heart were beating outside his body. A mug slipped from his hand, and his eyes went on fire. He wore jackets and sweaters in the apartment even though it was warm. I

My Life as an Animal

thought he should tell Cortez about the changes. He said, "I know how to take care of myself." By the third week of October, after routine blood work, he was readmitted to the hospital. His kidneys were clogged, and calcium was building in his blood.

The elevated calcium meant his bones were breaking down. Plasma cells produce antibodies. A normal person has hundreds of different antibodies, but in the case of multiple myeloma, one plasma cell clone takes over and suppresses the growth of other cells. The result—due to the insufficiency of red blood cells, white blood cells, and platelets—is exhaustion, pallor, infection, bruising, nosebleeds, and internal hemorrhaging. Gardner's tumor cell was proving too aggressive for the chemo to contain.

He died in Lenox Hill Hospital on December 17, 1990. He spent his last two months there. Since then I have relived the events many times, the last place I smelled him. In the days when he could hold down food, his daughter and I shopped for him at Zabar's and Fairway. Candace had her father's fair skin, thick hair, and extravagant blue eyes, and she, too, was an artist. She visited Gardner every day, stretching out beside him, the way I did. We were the same age. Early on, she had been unhappy about our relationship, but now we were a team. One day outside his room she said, "All my friends fell in love with my dad. He was Peter Pan. Everyone wanted to be at our house. There were no rules."

On Christmas day, a week after Gardner's death, I dreamed I was walking up Broadway, striding along with a feather duster, and the plumes began escaping. By the time I reached Columbia, only a few scraggly shreds remained, and then the wand leapt out of my hand and slipped down a sewer grate. A few weeks before this dream, Candace had dreamed of her father as a feather and wondered what it meant. I said, "Maybe he wasn't earthbound. Maybe you were thinking of his hair flying in the wind or of his brushstrokes." When I woke up, I saw how close the word *feather* is to *father*.

Some days Gardner improved. It's strange to record this because in memory the slide down is inexorable. He still believed the chemo would buy him time. I believed it, too. There wasn't anything else to believe. During these months I felt clearer than at any other time in my life. I was sad, but I knew what to do.

By early November, Gardner's kidney function had improved. He was eating, and his muscles were steadier. A catheter was inserted into his chest to draw blood and deliver drugs directly into his jugular vein. But a few days later, as a new round of chemo began, his calcium spiked again and his lungs filled with fluid. He was placed in the ICU, and he began to hallucinate. He thought he had been kidnapped to New Mexico and a woman had run him over with her truck. He thought she was in the next bed, and he was afraid. I wondered if he preferred this nightmare to reality.

He would fight his way back and after seventeen days leave the ICU. Afterward, he could walk only with assistance, and his skin was a wrinkled suit. One day I arrived at his room to find two nurses with tight faces mopping the floor. Gardner had called for help and no one had come. He had gotten out of bed, started to shit, and fallen hard in the mess. I told the nurses they could leave. Gardner was on the toilet. He rested his stick arms on my shoulders, and I moved him to the shower and onto a chair. A few days earlier, he had felt too weak to wipe his ass and had asked me to do it. A simple request, like, "Could you bring me a glass of water?" Now, with shit even in his hair, the scene was so sad it was almost funny. Gardner did not complain or apologize. He turned his face to the water without shame.

By the end of the month, he was readmitted to the ICU, his pulse having slowed. He was vomiting, and his lungs needed suctioning every hour. He dreamed he was in a warehouse of the dead where zombies were eating people. He was afraid he would be eaten next, and he did not want to die alone. I said, "You won't." If I left him for an hour, he thought it was days.

On December 11, he was placed on a respirator. A thick tube extended from his mouth to his lungs and rested against his vocal cords, so he could not speak. One afternoon I read him an article about Eric Fischl, placing glasses on his nose so he could look at paintings set in India. In one work, a woman was on the steps of a temple. Another painting was of a cow. For a few moments, we were immersed in color and light, but Gardner began reaching for the respirator, his eyes ablaze, his lips working around the tube, which was too wide for him even to mouth words. He could nod and squeeze my hand, but he was too disoriented to tap out words on an alphabet board.

I said, "Are you saying you want the tube out of your mouth?" He nodded, grabbing at it. I held his hands and said he would not be able to breathe without it. He let out a silent moan, and this moment, with Gardner cut off even from words, seemed the cruelest so far.

His sons came to visit. They touched him and spoke to him, but they did not want to remember him this way. The uric acid that would poison him was mounting, and on December 16 he fell unconscious. His lips were drawn back in a grimace, yet he was himself in the vehemence. His brows arched delicately. His eyes were still that crazy blue. I could not tell if his frail attempt to hold my hand was a function of the swelling or a desire to touch.

We seemed like figures in a pageant. The patient making secret bargains in hopes of being the miraculous exception. The doctors unable to pronounce a patient hopeless, even when treatment is futile. The house staff letting off steam with gallows humor. All of us chanting, "If there is a possibility of extending life, shouldn't we try?" "Oh, yes," we all said, "Yes, yes," because there is nothing else to say when the patient burns to live.

So we pressed on, reciting the litany of tests. Calcium, BUN, creatinine, red count, white count, blood gasses. We hung on the numbers as if they were talismanic. We charted the drugs. Lasix, Bactrim, dopamine, Compazine, the chemo brews. Each day a new procedure. X-rays, scans, enemas, catheters, biopsies, suctioning, tube feeding, bronchoscopies. No one said, "This is done," and Gardner did not want to be set free. He wanted three extra months, three extra weeks, three extra minutes. Four days before the end, doctors attached a dialysis pump to Gardner, but he ripped it out of his veins.

After he died, I met an oncologist who said, "You can't let someone bleed to death or die of an untreated infection. If therapeutic options remain, it is fair to try aggressively to reverse complications. Sometimes you think you are going to lose, and then you are surprised. I had a patient who was eighty-three and had always done for himself. The other doctors thought he was finished. I said, 'Fuck that,' and I worked on him for five months, and he left the hospital. He came back a few months later and did die. His heart gave out. But he didn't want to give up, and he appreciated the extra time. The peaceful death is a fallacy. Cancer beats the shit out of you. A good oncologist can buy good time. But multiple myeloma is humbling. Early detection and treatment don't

My Life as an Animal

necessarily affect its course. The doctor's role devolves to comforting, and most doctors don't want to admit that is all they can do. It feels like an invasion to them."

When Gardner was in the hospital, I worried he would die while I was washing dishes or applying lipstick. I told myself to take cabs. I worried he felt abandoned if I wasn't there. He didn't always remember when people came. Near the end I asked him if Candace had come that day, and he shook his head no, but later she told me she had visited. Sometimes when Gardner looked at me I thought he was saying, "Why are you standing there? Save me." I told Candace. I said, "I think he is angry at me for failing him." She said, "Are you angry with him?" I said, "No." She said, "Well, that's just as reasonable as thinking he could be angry with you. He is living in his body, as he always has. All he is thinking is, I feel pain, I feel uncomfortable, get this thing off me." She sounded just like him.

At the end, I wanted never to leave the hospital. Each morning when I woke up, I flashed to a scene in Alaska, where I had traveled the summer before, covering the Exxon oil spill. When I was in Homer, I would call Gardner from the porch of a health food store that smelled of the granola, yeast, and honey he would mix into what he called his morning "mortar." I could see him curled up on his couch. I was afraid of the bush planes I had to fly in in order to reach oiled beaches and injured animals. I was afraid of many things during the time I knew Gardner, and he would say, "I have no fear for you."

On December 17, I arrived at the hospital early. At two, a doctor said Gardner would die that day. The only sign of life was an ear that twitched when I said his name directly into it. His body was so swollen with fluid his shriveled arms were inflated again. He was running a fever of one hundred and five, and a cool blanket had been ordered. The tube leading to his stomach had been suctioning blood for days, pint after pint. How was this possible? His blood pressure was low, although his pulse was steady. When his pulse grew either very slow or very rapid, it would signal he was dying.

People had been arriving all day. It must have been five when Evelyn poked her head into Gardner's room and darted out again. She said she did not want to see him this way and asked if we could get coffee. Everyone said, "Go." A little while later my friend Carrie searched the café where we were sitting but oddly did not see us. Maybe my back was to the door. Maybe I was leaning into Evelyn.

She was seeing a man after a long time on her own. They had sex, and they argued. As she spoke, I remembered there was a world outside the hospital. She had years ago discarded me as an intimate friend. It was my fault. It was no one's fault. She had started a reading group I was not invited to join. I learned about it from a man who was a member. The man sat next to me at a bar with an embarrassed smile. I asked why he thought I had not been included. He was a well-published writer whose work I admired, balding and beginning to stoop. He said, "Maybe she doesn't think you're smart enough." I thought, Well, anyway, you think that.

Evelyn was here now, out of attachment or obligation, and I held on to the balloon of her, rising up, and I saw my life with Gardner, and we looked like ants scurrying along. We looked like comrade ants. Night after night of walking and holding each other. Sitting across from Evelyn, her eyes narrowing to slits, I remembered the surprise party she and Gardner had thrown for my thirty-fifth birthday. I had believed she was my special friend, and her presence at this passage made me hope for her again. I felt the future rushing in, a tunnel of cold air in which voices whispered excitedly about solitude and loss. A waiter kept refilling my cup, and then I saw an hour had passed.

I raced back to the hospital. The elevator smelled of disinfectant and fear. When the door opened, the head nurse was there holding a box of tissues. She said Gardner's pulse had suddenly slowed. "There was hardly any warning, which is odd because his heart was strong." She handed me a tissue and said, "This always happens. People sit for days, and then they step away for a few minutes, and the person dies."

I went to him, now free of machines. A cotton bonnet was tied over his head to keep his jaw from slipping to his chest. I kissed him. His face was still warm. His hands felt the way they had in life. I sat by his side, and for a long time there wasn't much difference between the way he had looked before death and now. I did not forgive myself for letting him die alone. I never will.

Candace entered and we cried. We held each other. Later we would take a taxi to Riverside Chapel and arrange the cremation in a room so gilded and ornate, we would laugh. We would feel drunk, our turtlenecks sticking to our skin. Candace would sign the forms as her mother, Frances Flynn, because Gardner, it would turn out, had not gotten around to signing his divorce papers. Weeks later I would visit Gardner's oncologist, and I would watch her hustle from the examining room, to the waiting room, to the phone. I would look into her dark eyes as she described a typical, fifteen-hour day. She would confide her marriage was strained. She would say ninety percent of her patients died in her care. She would say of Gardner's case that in all her years treating bone marrow cancer she had not seen so many tumors form.

I would say how much I thought about him, and she would say, "He hears you. He knows what you're feeling." I would say, "He can't hear anything. He doesn't know anything. Dead is dead." She would say, "You really believe that?" I would say, "Yes." But now, in the hospital, I sat beside him until his face grew waxen and stiff.

AS I REACHED THE BORDER OF WASHINGTON SQUARE Park, Evelyn called and invited me to her place. As I made my way there I thought about the many times I had passed her building, glancing up at her windows and wondering who she was talking to. How many years had it been since I had stood before her elevator, with its worn patch of carpet, and strolled down the hall to her door? It opened, and I said, "You look beautiful." She said, "So do you." I said, "Of course." We laughed.

She sat in her old armchair, and I took the couch, and as her face grew animated, she was as beautiful as ever with her slanted eyes and smooth skin. In a corner of the living room sat a glass-topped table Gardner had made for me and I had given to her after he died and I moved his granite table to my apartment. A vase of red amaryllis blossoms reflected off the surface, and I could see Gardner in the bright flashes. He was on the floor, nose to nose with Sasha, holding the dog's ears and saying, "What's going on in that dog suit?"

Evelyn's apartment was orderly and calm, and several books faced out of the shelves—*The Second Sex*, *Native Son*, *My Dog Tulip*. She said, "They comfort me." Her affair with the arguing man had fizzled out some years later. She said, "Loneliness is a sickness. You don't say, 'I'm lonely' casually, the way you do 'I'm hungry' or 'I feel like taking a walk.'" She said, "These days when I go out, I look for a stranger to assist. It makes me like myself more."

I thought about the difference between loneliness, which deadens thought, and aloneness, which stirs reflection. Several months after Gardner died, I saw the movie *Henry and June*, based on the diaries of Anaïs Nin. The film chronicles Nin's affairs with Henry Miller and Miller's flamboyant wife, June. The setting is Paris in the 1920s, and the movie is sexy—girls with girls and girls with boys. Nin ventures into the demimonde, thinking she is going out on a limb. At the same time, whenever she feels anxious or threatened, she retreats to her rich husband, Hugo, who calls her pussy willow. Henry is conceited and bombastic, but he lives without a safety net. In the last scene, Nin weeps, claiming she is grieving for the end of her affair with Henry, but as I watched tears slide down the cheeks of the actress, I thought, No, Nin is crying because Henry is a better writer than she is, and he is a better writer because he is not trying to look good.

I felt peaceful in Evelyn's apartment and asked what she was working on. She thought for a moment and said, "Maybe a memoir of my friendship with Albert." I said, "Do it." She said, "Why?" I said, "We need books about friendship." In the early days of the women's movement, we believed friends were family, but they are not family. Friendship is more delicate. You have to be careful with friends. She said that in order to write the book she would need to locate her love for Albert. She said, "When we're talking and laughing, I feel connected, but afterward I don't trust that the feelings are real." She said she and Albert could rely on each other, but she worried they did not hold each other in the tender, excited regard she was always looking for.

Leaving Gardner

She had recently written a piece about anarchism and had come to believe there was such a thing as an anarchist temperament. She thought there were people who burned all the time in an oven of rage, and sometimes the rage became attached to a social cause. She thought the disposition might be genetic, and I remembered the night we had met, brought together by a mutual friend. Evelyn had been cruel to the host. They had argued—something about Marilyn Monroe—and I had sided with her. I wish I had not. She was a wolverine, and I was a baby wolverine, bouncing around the kill.

She asked what I had written lately, and I mentioned a piece about *Swimming in a Sea of Death*, the memoir by David Rieff about his mother, Susan Sontag. I said Rieff felt bad about giving his mother's death a bad review, and Evelyn laughed. I looked out the window. Light was draining over the zigzagging streets of the West Village. A sliver of river glinted through condos that had risen up over the years. Twinkling streetlights were coming on, and Evelyn looked cozy in her chair. Stacked on the coffee table were books she was reading for research and review. She didn't own a TV.

She had heard I had met a man who taught in Arizona and that I was spending long periods there. She had taught in Tucson for many years, feeling like a Chekhov character exiled to the provinces. She looked at me kindly, as if to say, Rejoice in connection. It is the best reason for being alive. She said, "You are doing the right thing. Of course you have to be there."

I felt our old rhythm returning, and I wondered if friendship could be revived. Perhaps, if you adjusted your position a little or felt more compassion for the people who are on fire. Maybe heaven, hell, and purgatory are metaphors for the impressions we leave on other people—the more happiness we produce, the larger our reward. I felt the distance that had grown between us, too. We did not know each other's stories anymore. Sometimes it flashes on you that you have traveled far or someone has traveled far from you. You think you know where you live and where the shops are down the street and who will ring up your groceries, and then one day you wake up in a different city and the light is unfamiliar. Cold doesn't sting. Heat doesn't burn. The air smells like a tree you don't know the name of. You don't know if you have come to a better place or a worse place, but you know you have moved away.

I often think about the Lydia Davis story "Happy Memories," in which the narrator considers what makes a happy memory. She says it requires feeling warmth toward a person who will retain you happily in their thoughts and also that nothing subsequently can happen that reverses the goodwill. Twenty-five years ago Gardner and I climbed Mount Monadnock in New Hampshire. The trek was trickier than I had expected. We hiked for many hours, and at the icy top Sasha slipped and nearly toppled to his death. Because Gardner caught him, the memory remains a happy one.

I peered into Evelyn's office. On her desk were neat piles of notes, and tacked on the wall was a schedule of projects. I had read her books over the years and been struck by how, increasingly, she found ways to appreciate her subjects, even when she was critical of them.

That night I dreamed I was a young man in an asylum, intense and nervous, and my name was on a list of people who would die. I circulated among the more mobile patients. One was a man with feathery hair, shorter than me and muscular, a real man I depended on because he knew about the outside world. I was shivering on a road and rain was dripping down my neck. We were buying clothes on St. Mark's Place, and clerks began to whisper about us. We ran out of the store. We ran to the countryside and threw ourselves backward into a field of snow. It was our only escape, and we held our breath under the whiteness that was almost like death. Then the snow became a sea, and we swam to an island. If I stayed there long enough, everyone from my past would show up. There was not a person, living or dead, tender or wounding, I did not want to see.

I LIKE TALKING TO YOU

A few nights ago I felt drowsy until it was time for bed. Then I was awake and took an Ambien. I lay on my pillow, prepared to slide under, as air-conditioning slapped my cheek just this side of too much. At three thirty I got up to raise the thermostat, tripped on a pillow, and broke the fall with my hand. In the morning on our walk, Richard kissed my hand and said, "I was thinking about the time when you will be dotty and fall down a lot." I said, "Why do you think I will be dotty before you?" Then I remembered I was four years older than him. The trail was rocky, the stones jutting up. Richard was thinking about the difference in our ages when I did not know he was thinking about it, and I wondered what else he was thinking. It was like we were in a train, sitting face-to-face, and while he was seeing the future I was looking at the past. I said, "I fell because of the Ambien." I said, "There are people half my age who can't keep up with me." But I was thinking the same thing he was.

Richard's parents had recently died: his father of stomach cancer and his mother six months later from multiple strokes. She had been on another planet, but still she was gone, and the suddenness of both deaths was violent. Richard was grieving, although you would not know it to look at him. There was no lamentation.

We were just back from a trip to England, where we had trailed through a graveyard with Nicky, one of Richard's sisters, as she scissored between mossy headstones, some tilting toward each other like drunken friends. She had pointed out the resting places of Brooks ancestors, and Richard had smiled softly until, at the end of a shrubbery-banked lane, he stared down blankly at a small granite cube that housed both portions of parental ashes. Nicky had tossed them together, much the way the couple had lived, and I thought this unfair to Mary. Richard's father had been a doting but hovering presence in his wife's life, and I thought she was owed a bit of privacy at the end. When Richard and I were alone, he said, "My father was born on Barkby Road, and now he's ended up on Barkby Road." He shuddered. I squeezed his hand.

Tonight, in Arizona, we were joining a couple for dinner. As I got ready, I remembered how much I like restaurants, and I felt my life would be measly without Richard. I saw myself rattling around my apartment in New York, my face crumbling along with the paint. I went to Richard's office and said the thing about my life being measly. He said, "My life would be measly, too." I said, "Why?" He said, "I like talking to you." I said, "I like talking to you, too."

The day before we had been driving around to Target and Whole Foods. We stopped at a Starbucks. Most of the seats were occupied by wedding planners and chubby, sad-eyed brides-to-be. Richard and I found a table and wrote in our notebooks. Every so often I looked at his abrupt nose and smooth cheeks. After we finished writing, I said, "I once sat next to Shari Lewis on a plane." I could see myself in the win-

My Life as an Animal

dow seat, and I could see Shari to my left, her hair a nimbus of curls. She didn't look much older than when, as a child, I had watched her on TV, Shari and her sock puppet, Lamb Chop. Even then I had found it disturbing that an animal was named after a cut of its own meat. Richard said, "Suzanne sat next to Shari Lewis on a plane. They had a long conversation and exchanged emails." I said, "Do you think I stole her memory?" I could see Shari's foundation makeup caking in little creases around her eyes. I said, "Is it possible we both sat next to Shari Lewis on a plane?" Richard set down his cup and said, "No." He said, "In language you can steal things that can't really be stolen." I wasn't sure what this meant. In the car, he said, "You look younger when you're happy." I looked in the right-hand mirror and saw a Spielberg alien with a pointy chin and large, hollowed eyes.

On our way to dinner, Richard said, "I'm a moody person." He was reading a book about Byron, and he thought he shared something of the clubfooted poet's malcontent. I said, "Okay," meaning yes, you are! He was silent for a while. We arrived early in order to write in a café. He sat with his arms crossed and said, "I can't sit around waiting for grief to come, if it ever will. Maybe I should read a book about bereavement, *Death for Dummies*, or I could check out Barnes and Noble to see if there's a kit that could help me miss my parents, like there are kits that teach you to juggle, or learn rock guitar, or throw a horoscope." I said, "You throw pots, not horoscopes." He ordered a glass of wine, saying, "I need to lift my spirits." I did not say the thing I was thinking about using wine to lift your spirits, and while I was keeping my mouth shut I thought about the benefits of silence. There is something about language that hurts the thing it describes. After not speaking for a while, I worried I was turning English, which felt vaguely antisemitic and made me miss my parents.

We were having dinner with the ex-wife of Richard's best friend and Quinn's new boyfriend, another Brit by chance, who was visiting her. When we arrived at the restaurant, she did not look like a person whose lover had crossed an ocean and a continent to be with her. Her hair was long and curtained her cheeks with their saddle of freckles. She was tall and slim, one of those women who look like a girl until you notice little lines on the forehead and around the mouth. When she excused herself to go to the bathroom, I followed her and said, "Quinn, you look unhappy." She said, "I'm fine. I'm having a wonderful time."

The next week she would invite Richard and me for drinks and say, "I need a therapist to get over this guy." She would say she bought her own plane tickets and waited in hotel rooms for her lover to steal away from his wife. Even so, she would thrill to the tale, and I would remember times I had raced to an airport to meet a stranger. Quinn would say, "I met a brilliant man online, and I'm important to him. We text and Skype several times a day." She would finish her drink and say, "Where can it go? What am I doing?" I would say, "You are exciting yourself. You are doing what we do to have a life."

On the way home from this drink, Richard would say, "I don't understand what she's doing. She's in love with a man who doesn't love her back." I would say, "Desire fulfilled is desire destroyed." He would say, "Do you mean you need to be uncertain of a person in order to be hot for them?" I would say, "I don't know what I mean." He would say, "I don't need that." I would say, "Okay, but Quinn doesn't want to be fifty and alone in Arizona. She fears this frustrating affair is the best she is going to get. When she looks back on her life, she wants the memory to go through her like an ax. What does anyone want to remember but the times we were out of control?" Richard would say, "I don't want to remember that." I would say, "You don't have to."

At the restaurant, Quinn's boyfriend did not drape his arm around her shoulder, or speak in her ear, or describe their time together in the desert. It was as if he was auditioning for a job and Quinn was his agent. It was as if he was embarrassed to have come so far for a few nights of sex. He was tall and gray haired. He could have passed for her uncle. He mentioned a book he had published about the Brontës, and I drifted to the scene in *Jane Eyre* where Rochester implores Jane to live as his wife, even though he is still married to Bertha Mason, the mad woman living in his attic. Rochester says, "Who will care?" meaning Jane is an orphan. Jane, who was about to marry Rochester, is wearing her wedding dress. Now, having learned of Bertha's existence, she says, "I will care," and you thrill at her self-possession, even though you have to ask yourself, In real life has anyone ever made Jane's choice?

Quinn's boyfriend mentioned having been at Oxford, and I could hear his plummy vowels drilling into Richard's head. Richard's vowels have a northern, Beatles' lilt. He says *toof* for *tough* and *soofer* for *suffer*. It is hard not to imitate him, and it makes you understand how Linda McCartney wound up sounding like a fake Beatle. After the meal, Quinn's boyfriend paid the check, and the four of us walked along a canal in the fiery air. We chatted about nothing because no one was saying what they felt. Suddenly Richard offered to connect Quinn's boyfriend to some of his colleagues in Leeds. Quinn's boyfriend had made a documentary about archaeology in Yorkshire, and Richard said, "I'll give Simon a call about setting up a screening." Richard looked surprised, as if birds were flying out of his mouth.

On the drive home, I was at the wheel, and Richard looked out the window. We cruised along a road lined with resort hotels and strip malls. He said, "You're driving outside the lane." I eased over to where he thought the car should be and didn't mention the thing he does when I drive. I don't mind it as much as a person should because it makes him seem crazier than me. He said, "I'm just trying to be helpful." I laughed with a snort. He said, "Be careful." I said, "Of what? You have to say, 'Be careful of the rabbit' or 'Look out for the truck fishtailing on the left.' Otherwise I don't know what you're talking about." He said, "Don't raise your voice. When you raise your voice, I can't listen to you." I said, "You are missing your family." He said, "What do you mean?" I said, "In your house, no one was allowed to yell. Everyone said, 'That's right, of course,' while thinking, You are a gigantic idiot. In your family you had to act like it was the Blitz every day and displeasure was rude and unpatriotic." He said, "You don't know anything about my family." I said, "Okay."

We drove past towering palms, some banded with tiny lights that made them look festive and displaced. Richard said, "I didn't need to make that offer to Geoff." He bit one of his fingers. "Remember the scene in *Lear* when Gloucester is blind, and he thinks he's on the edge of a cliff when, really, he's only on a mound of sand? I often feel that way. I'm trying to feel the edge. I know I'm supposed to be generous, but I offer too much and then I resent the person for it. My parents were trying to sort this out their whole lives, and they never even managed to feel safe away from home. Poor old Mum and Dad." I said, "Poor old Mum and Dad."

My Life as an Animal

The next day we walked in the desert, and after a while I said, "I'm hungry." Richard fished in his bag and handed me a packet of nuts he had been carrying around. He popped a few in his mouth and said, "These nuts are interesting." I ate one and said, "These nuts are rancid." He said, "*Rancid* is too strong a word." I said, "Nuts get rancid. That's what nuts do." Later we passed a saguaro that had dried in the shape of a human figure. Its arms were raised and its back was stooped. I said, "It looks like my mother." Richard said, "By the time you are seventy-five, you will be bent over, too. You will look just like her and scream, 'Get away from me' and shake your fists." I said, "You could find someone younger." He said, "I could, couldn't I?" I said, "Do it soon. I'd rather have my heart broken now than later." He said, "Why?"

THIN

In 1998 a man I was in love with ended things with me, and I flew to Los Angeles to give readings and stay in the house of a sadomasochist my friend Ruby was dating. I was thin. Ruby arranged my housing and the venues where I would read. She was a good friend, although she once told me we had the same ferrety, Jewish faces. After that, whenever I looked in the mirror, I could see what she meant. I read at Beyond Baroque with a writer who gave me a sweater for my birthday. The collar was made of feathers, and I wore it for the softness. I had not eaten much during the time I was with Sammy. I was always worried he wouldn't show up.

The sadomasochist went by the name Jaz. He was small with a closely cropped head and sad eyes. He and Ruby had met online, and he lived in a cottage behind a house that faced a nondescript, noir-looking L.A. street. One of the rooms in Jaz's house was locked, and I wondered if it contained a dungeon. It could have been where he tossed his dirty socks, but the dungeon came to mind. I was generally interested in dungeons, but now they reminded me too much of my relationship with Sammy. At the airport I rented a car, and when I arrived at Jaz's place he reviewed a list of instructions for the care of his belongings and cat. Like I was supposed to be grateful for his sullen house and chipped plates! I said, "Okay."

Ruby was excited by the sexual things he did with her, but in time she found them funny. She said, "Perhaps the drive to hurt the body always turned people on and religion and sacrifice were invented so we could keep doing it." This idea appealed to me. It made sex something you weren't responsible for. I was not yet at the laughing stage about Sammy. Jaz asked me to drive him to the airport. He was jittery in the car, not sexy or scary, and it was like catching a magician out of costume. He taught people to make self-promotional videos, and I wondered about the relationship between sadomasochism and self-promotion, and it occurred to me in both situations you followed a script. In the mornings, I would tune in the financial news on Jaz's enormous TV and watch the numbers whisk along as if on their way to important appointments. Most days, I had no destination, and Los Angeles was a perfect place for this, since I did not know how to drive from point A to point B.

At my last meeting with Sammy, he came to my apartment to return the things I had given him. I said, "Keep them," although I now miss my mug from the Soho Grand Hotel. I spent so much time counting the ways he could not love me, it was a job. He sat beside me on the couch, and I felt the hairs on his legs. He was so happy to be free, he became aroused.

After Jaz returned from his trip, I stayed with Ruby in her stucco house. It was perched on a hill that was slowly slipping down to the road below. A glass wall looked out to a patio banked with oleander and bougainvillea. I slept in the little guest cottage halfway down the hill. In the cottage, Ruby had once waited for Jaz while kneeling naked over a bowl of ice cubes. He was on his way to see her and wanted to imagine her with nothing better to do. She was accommodating. It was one of the reasons I liked her, too. We sat on her white bed. She said, "Time is long and grief is like tricking with a stranger." Those were not her exact words. She said, "Work is the center of our lives. That is who we are. Work and friendship." Was work the center of my life? I could feel the house slipping. Something was moving, and I saw that the loss of Sammy was bigger than the relationship had been. Ruby said, "Love is *Midsummer Night's Dream.* Your demon lover turns out to be an ass." I did not think this was true in every case, but her voice was musical, and I felt myself melting into the scenery. And as my friend gazed with kindness at my swollen eyes, I began to feel like eating.

WOLF OR DOG

On Thanksgiving 2002, Ruby invited a crowd to her house in the Adirondacks. When I arrived, I learned that no one knew how to cook. I started to chop and sauté things, although Ruby would not have minded if people hacked off chunks of raw turkey and cooked them on sticks in the fireplace. As I worked, she leaned against the counter and chatted. She was wearing a plaid kilt and a sweater with a fake fur collar and cuffs. It was as if I were changing a flat on her car on a lonely stretch of road, and she was flirting.

I cooked sausage with celery and onions for stuffing. Ruby's husband was on the couch, as far from the kitchen as he could get. He was writing an essay, and I hated him. Ruby said, "I read somewhere that wolves were suckled by human mothers. Do you think this is true?" I said, "Romulus and Remus." She said, "Romulus and Remus were human babies suckled by a wolf. Besides, they weren't real." She picked a piece of sausage from the pan and popped it in her mouth. I said, "Wolves became dogs by eating scraps at the campfires of humans. Wolves basically domesticated themselves." Ruby said, "That is the saddest thing I have ever heard." I said, "Yes, but some wolves went on being wolves."

Guests trickled in: boys with tattoos and crested hairdos; girls in high heels and cropped jackets. The girls were the girlfriends of the boys, who were former students of Ruby's husband. The girls drifted into the kitchen with Ruby and me. The boys gathered in the living room and sprawled on the red Moroccan carpet as Ruby's husband delivered an impromptu lecture on the brutal legacies of colonial power. His name was Etienne Sobel. He was a famous academic. He wore black clothes and silver jewelry. His hair was chopped up, punk-style.

Etienne and Ruby were an on-again-off-again couple who dwelt in assorted apartments and houses they owned. The Adirondacks house was furnished with rickety, mismatched, yard-sale chairs and lamps as well as mementos from their travels. In one photograph they stand in front of a Turkish mosque, squinting at the sun. A shaft of light stabs the space between their bodies. In another photograph they lean against a crumbling wall in Serbia. Ruby was free to see other men, a freedom that felt like an imposition because she did not really want to. She would call me crying at the end of one of her affairs, and I would say, "Some people fall in love with the way you are aroused by them and then feel cheated by who you really are." I knew this from personal experience.

The girlfriends of the boys asked if they could help in the kitchen, and I gave them jobs. The boys did not enter the kitchen. Ruby heated a bowl of soup for Etienne and placed it on the coffee table with a spoon and a cloth napkin. She brought him tea. I rolled out dough for pies and sliced apples. She said, "How do you know how to do these things?" I said, "I watched Julia Child."

By the time the turkey was done and the last cold light of the afternoon was slipping down the living room walls, the

My Life as an Animal

girls and Ruby set the table and carried chairs to the place settings while the boys popped cans of beer and warmed their feet by the crackling fire. During the meal, Etienne did not rouse himself to carry food to the table or return plates to the sink. He was thin and ate furtively, as if food was important one moment and trivial the next. I did not know why, apart from his fame, Ruby was with him. I did not know why anyone was with anyone.

The girls and I kept the meal moving between the kitchen and dining room. After the main course was served, I sliced the pies and scooped ice cream onto plates. Then I went up to each woman and said, "Let's get out of here." They said okay, no questions asked, and seven or eight of us packed into the station wagon I had borrowed from a friend and drove to a splintery roadhouse with torn leather stools. The only people there were loners without families and drunks with sheepskin coats and hats with flaps. I ordered a drink.

We talked to one another and livened up the place with our runaway energy. Half an hour later the boys arrived, and Etienne glided sullenly across the wood floor, his biker boots squeaking. He said to Ruby, "What is going on here?" He spoke in a soft, babyish voice. His eyebrows were raised, and I felt a little afraid and a little go fuck yourself.

Ruby had thick red hair and a waifish figure. She shrugged and smiled then went to the jukebox and played a Rolling Stones song. She danced around, making people feel good, and I was reminded of a story a student of mine once wrote. The story didn't seem to be about anything until a character said, "What's the point of being beautiful if everyone can be?" The student thought beauty was defined by ugliness. She thought there was such a thing as beauty and ugliness. I asked her if she thought she was beautiful, and she said, "Yes,

I have a kind of beauty. Everyone has a kind of beauty." I said, "If everyone has a kind of beauty, where is the ugliness?" This was the question I thought I should be asking myself, although I did not want to.

Ruby whispered in Etienne's ear, and he came to where I was standing. We held drinks, our shoulders nearly touching. We seldom spoke to each other. I did not know how to talk to him. I said, "What does colonialism mean to you personally?" It was the wrong thing to ask, and I knew it. His eyes widened, and he said, "You don't need a personal involvement for a political position. You need a moral understanding." I said, "I was wondering what makes you care about the things you care about." I did not care. He folded his arms and leaned against the wall. I could feel the music vibrating through the floor. He closed his eyes and said, "When I was a child, the Nazis were occupying France, and as Jews my family had to flee Paris and disappear into the countryside. I was placed with farmers I did not know." I asked how old he was. He said, "Five." I asked if the farmers had been kind to him. He shook his head, and tears welled in his eyes. I felt like I was supposed to like him.

Ruby floated over and said to me, "Let's dance." I wanted to kiss her. She said, "Don't look so serious." I said, "A wolf ate my sense of humor." She said, "A wolf would not eat something so insubstantial." She slipped her arm through mine and said, "What should we dance to?" I went to the jukebox and chose "The Passenger" by Iggy Pop. The music began to thrum, and we circled each other's necks, our faces close.

Iggy's voice was gravelly and insinuating. He was a kid in his room, bare chested and free. He sang about a ride through the city at night, with stars that were his and an ocean road that was his. He knew his life was drifting by and that soon he would die, but he says to his girl, "Let's drive. Let's live." I danced around with Ruby, feeling less alone in the world.

The next morning she came into my room and slid under the covers. She was wearing a T-shirt and panties, and I felt the softness of her arms and legs. She said, "Do you like Etienne more, now?" I said, "Yes." It was a lie and it was not a lie. She said, "He's angry at you. He thinks you made him cry on purpose." She laughed her silvery, devil's laugh. I said, "You like being in the middle." She said, "People like my books more than his books, and I feel bad for him." I said, "The fifties called, and they want their decade back."

A toilet flushed. Feet clomped down the stairs and the smell of coffee wafted into the room. I said, "How do you feel about his sitting there last night and doing nothing?" She said, "The dinner was my idea. He thought he was doing enough by having people to the house." I said, "He didn't ask why we left." She said, "He knows and thinks it was stupid." I said, "Do you think it was stupid?" She stretched her arms over her head and said, "I don't think these things are as big a deal as you do." I said, "Why not?" She looked across at the window. The curtains were fluttering, and there was snow on the trees outside. She said, "His work changes the world." I said, "Even if it does, if he won't do his share at home, it means that what matters to us becomes less important among the changes we want to make. We have to go to the end of the line again. Don't you think we're supposed to be with men who get this?" She said, "I don't expect as much from men as you do."

I laughed, and I wondered what I did expect from men, and as the question formed I knew I would not get it, and it felt like knowing you would die before the end of the story, like a terminal patient cut off in the middle of a soap opera. I wondered how it would feel to be with a man like Etienne, who had power in the world and could help you circulate your ideas. But would he?

In one theory of the origin of language, our primate ancestors needed words to gather a group larger than their tribe in order to frighten away large predators from feeding sites. According to this theory, language and cooperation arrived together. At the same time, humans have tended to kill off the strangest and most creative individuals before they could pass along their genes. When I think about Ruby, I wonder which of us is more a wolf, able to go her own way, and which of us is more a circling dog.

ALOES

I am pulling up aloes in the front yard. The leaves are brown and frizzled, and ropy roots circle the cluster. They look like a bedraggled family herded into a small holding pen, and now I am feeling sorry for them. They have long, thick legs, like geoduck clams with their obscene siphons, and I toss them into a bin, clearing an eyesore, but as I extract a husky elder, emerald pups peek out among the spikes. Oh my god, there are babies!

They lift away with surprising ease. In Arizona, the ground is hard and roots spread along the surface, and you don't need a shovel, although I use one and accidentally chop up some pups. Aloes have barbed, razor edges you need gloves to protect you from, although hair-thin prickles burrow under your skin and are hard to dislodge. Buddhists say pain derives from interpretation. They mean inner pain. Whatever they mean, the concept is irritating.

Aloe pups grow attached to mother plants, and you have to pull them apart, same as anywhere. At eighty-nine, my mother says, "When I am gone, take a finger to remember me by." I say, "How will I get the meat off?" She says, "That's where the mice come in." And I see them nip, nipping her, and I remember a poisoned rat that came to die on our patio. Its fur was fluffy, its ears tiny trumpets, its nose a needle, really pointy, with whiskers on either side, delicate as eyelashes. For several hours the rat breathed slowly until finally it fell over, and I thought, Whatever you look at long enough comes to look like you. My mother says, "The next twenty years will speed by like a bullet, so make the most of them." I think, How do you decide in a moment to make the most of it?

I set the heartiest aloes along a stone ledge. Richard and I are working in the falling light, and I remember the first time we saw this house. We had been uncertain if we would stay in Arizona, and then Richard landed the teaching job he had always wanted. Realtors say people make up their minds about a house in thirty seconds, and that is how long we took. I remember the small nod of approval we exchanged as we swept across the shiny wood floors and took in the high stone wall. For a while we were shy with the garden, the way we had been slow to peel ourselves back for each other. In the desert winter is a brief grumble, but all it takes is a few cold nights for color to drain from bougainvilleas. Their bony limbs shiver, and you have to cut them back to stumps. You need the dispassion of a surgeon, so don't look to me for that. When the weather warms, glossy, heart-shaped leaves form and branches overreach again. Richard asks if I think he will be fired from his job. I say, "No." It is a question that has only one answer.

We hack away at the larger aloes, their stalks snaky and snarled. It is like coming upon a ruin, say Grey Gardens, produced by a radical form of letting go. It is like clearing sickness from a heart. As I sort the living from the dead, I get into a rhythm. It is like riding a train as the landscape sweeps by and you feel a sense of continuity because you are the one doing the looking.

I am crouched on the ground, and I remember a rendering of Lucy, our ancient ancestor. She was posed on a savanna near a watering hole, looking up over her shoulder, and her eyes were beady and suspicious but also soulful. She was crooking a finger, as if to say, "Come closer," and she looked like my mother. Well, she would, wouldn't she? The landscape of Arizona is a severe kind of blank people read into a strict, withholding father. That's why they see God in the desert, the same way they imagined love in the man who sat mutely at the kitchen table, holding a beer.

The roots of aloes are moist and fibrous and dark as coffee grounds. They look like a medium for the beginning of life and the end, and I remember a café in Great Barrington. It was behind a cheese store, and it was expensive in a casual way. A goat could walk in, but a cookie cost five dollars. Richard and I were imagining a life in this town. It was a game we played called "After Arizona," and I said, "Let's give it a rest," and a gleam came into his eyes.

There is a sort of horror in pulling up aloes. It's their failure to resist and take firm root, like a set of rotting teeth or the limbs of a scarecrow, and I remember driving with a man when I was twenty-five. He was ten years older than me, and we were having a little affair, and as we sped along, he made up a ditty that went, "Oh, half my life is over, and yet it's just begun." I proposed that our generation would be the last one to die, and his face paled and he shuddered, and I saw an outcrop shearing off from the mainland like a chunk of California coming loose from the San Andreas

Fault. We were moving out in a dolly shot. We were aloes on a ledge. This morning in bed, Richard said, "You could leave and never return." I said, "How likely is that?" He said, "Not very," but he was leaving room for me to disappear, and in that space I wanted him.

MARCO

For several years, Marco and I crossed paths at conferences and festivals. He was thick, planted, and meaty with the intelligence dogs reflect in their unmasked eyes and anxious brows. It was an absurd attraction. They are all absurd. He was ending a marriage and in love with another woman. I was fifty-eight and believed this kind of thing would not happen to me again. When has anything you thought about the future turned out right?

The thing about arousal is that when you are not feeling it, you forget how you exist in it. Marco was smoking at a table in a bar. I moved to sit beside him, and we began a conversation. Other people were there, but soon we were talking only to each other, or I was listening to him. He described an essay he was writing. I do not know what he said. I was watching his lips circle a cigarette and perch on the rim of his glass.

Another night we were on a train. I had been drinking but was clear. Marco drank a lot. He had a big problem, but like many drunks he was steady on his feet. He was reading an account by Walt Whitman of visiting wounded soldiers during the Civil War, and he liked the way Whitman eroticized the men's bodies. I was reminded of Florence Nightingale's similar attraction to soldiers maimed in the Crimea, the way her mind had drifted to the bodies of naked men. Marco, too, admired the fanatical founder of nursing, and as the train rattled through blustery darkness we discussed Nightingale's reforms of the British military and of public health in India. Sleeping passengers looked wrapped in the same dream, their heads thrown back, their throats soft and unguarded. I was slumped in my seat, looking up at Marco's puffy eyes.

We were separated for several months and then found ourselves together at a conference. Marco's body reminded me of the bodies of other men I had known, but I had also favored different kinds of bodies. I cannot say for sure it was his body, although when I was out of its range, my sense of myself returned. I preferred to be away from him, but that was not always possible. If I was near him, I became aroused and could not see or hear anything.

One day we were walking and he said, "Is something going to happen with us?" A sense of peace came over me, and I said no. He reminded me of a man I had known some years earlier, but Marco was crazier, more confident, more dependent on women. His hands and feet were wide and callused. I imagined cutting off the calluses in a tub. When I removed my clothes, I told myself to remember the room, the window, the flowers in a vase, although afterward I could not remember anything the way I had wanted to. I liked the parts of sex that did not have words and the parts that did, although afterward I could not tell the difference. There was a way Marco was both female and male. He cried easily, and his hair was long. I liked that he took risks, but I did not like his carelessness with me. Neither love, respect, nor knowledge has ever stripped me of my inhibitions.

My Life as an Animal

At this time, I was reading the erotic works of Georges Bataille, and I admired their lack of affect. The narrator of *Story of the Eye*, for example, relates scenes of absurd sexual activity busting through the fabric of everyday life. A frisky girl thrusts her naked behind into a bowl of milk. A young man, imagining the white buttocks of his paramour to be two, hard-boiled eggs, feels an impulse to piss on them. That sort of thing. The events in Bataille's stories unfold as if they *were* ordinary life, without apology or interpretation. The narrator's containment allows the reader to enter the story as if the story is about the reader.

You get something of this effect when you go to bed with a person you do not know. Marco was polite. He came from one of those backgrounds, and I could not guess what he was thinking. In theory I like imagining people's unspoken thoughts. In theory I like being wrong, along with other things I like only in theory, such as ambiguity.

One night Marco and I stayed up late. He was brooding about his faraway love. I was brooding about him. Everywhere I went, I scanned for his shape. We reviewed events of the week, recalling times we had felt estranged from each other and times we had felt connected, and I relaxed because we shared the habit of keeping notes. At three in the morning we walked into the California countryside. A lace of clouds moved swiftly over stars that illuminated the night. The ground was damp. An owl hooted as we came to a clearing beside a pond and flopped on the grass. The air smelled of earth. We wrapped our arms around each other like blankets.

Marco had grown up in Virginia with a minister father. God was real to him, although he no longer practiced religion. His specialty was seventeenth-century literature, and he was writing an essay about *Midsummer Night's Dream*. He said he liked Shakespeare's view of sex, where people are interchangeable. "In Shakespeare," he said, "you love the one you're with. Sex doesn't mean anything. It's passion that can ruin you, the way it does Marc Antony." He said, "Power, not sex, is what matters in Shakespeare."

I asked what he made of the beginning of *Midsummer Night's Dream*, when Hermia's father says, in effect, Either you marry the boy I pick for you, or I put you to death. The law says I can. Then Theseus backs him up, telling Hermia she should view her father as a god because he created her. She's merely wax, and it's up to him to spare or disfigure her.

Marco said, "The play salutes lovers in nature, where they escape these laws. Hermia disobeys her father, gets the boy she wants, and doesn't die. It's a celebration of fertility and marriage. It's a comedy." I said, "Some comedy. The women wind up married." He said, "The play is set in ancient Athens, by way of Elizabethan England, not in your head." He said, "Comedy is about not dying."

I knew what comedy was about. Comedy was something I happened to know about, and I was trying not to die here, as the sky blushed with rosy light. I was trying not to ruin a tender moment, although that bird had left the branch. We stood and brushed off our clothes. The other women in Marco's life came up, as they invariably did. I thought of one as The Mother and the other as The Magician. "Who am I?" I asked unwisely, as we tramped over bumpy ground. He thought for a moment and shot me a sideways look. He said, "You're my Jew."

It felt like hearing mean laughter through a thin wall. It felt like light breaking into a dream. Freud maintained that dreams contain a secret wish, no matter how disturbing their content.

My Life as an Animal

I asked what he meant. I had not talked to Marco about being a Jew. He paused and said, "The way you ask questions. The way you have sex."

Was there a Jewish way to ask questions, a Jewish way to have sex? Perhaps if you were not a Jew it might seem there was, although what he was saying looked like a category mistake. It looked like he was saying, This person is a Jew. This person behaves in certain ways. Therefore those ways are Jewish. I wondered what category mistakes I had made about Marco, but I did not care. His category was sex, and that, no matter what he said, did not change.

GOAT

Twice a day I walk a three-mile course on a country road. Bushes and trees, magenta pea blossoms, and a rose of Sharon volunteer grow beside the blacktop. I am in rural Virginia in the Blue Ridge Mountains, where it seldom rains. Sleepy houses are set back from the road, and people sit out on lawn chairs and wave to passersby. I wave back. Dogs sniff around as you pass them. Some people are afraid of the dogs and carry sticks.

A wooden church is propped on a hill, and a little further along a herd of goats tear around or stare out. Cows graze in a farmer's field and beyond is a pond, and when you take in the scene as the road sweeps up, you see rolling hills in the background and puffy clouds above, and the scene suggests the English countryside. It is a little like a Constable, and it makes me happy.

One day I pass a goat who maahhs. It sounds like he is saying, "Hello." I maahh back. He maahhs again, only this time his voice rises at the end, and it sounds like he is saying, "Don't leave me." I return this maahh, walking fast, but then I see he has locked his head in the fence by his horns. I go to him through tall grass and brambles. He is standing with his head turned to the side.

No car passes now, but often as I walk a car or a truck will stop and the driver will ask, "Are you all right?" Sometimes the driver is a man, sometimes a woman. I am walking alone, a woman on a road. That's all it takes.

There is a man at the artist colony where I am staying who practices letting go of anger, and we have become friends. He has a white goatee and kind eyes that look out from rimless specs. He says, "There is a text in the *I Ching* called 'Releasing the Goat.' It means your stubbornness." I hold the goat's head, and he stops crying. His face is white with black markings, and two horns sweep back from his forehead. The horns are extensions of bone, and they feel strong and hard. I don't think I have ever held the horns of a goat, and I realize I have wanted to be close to these animals since I first saw them. I wonder what it would feel like to have horns of my own, and then I remember that is what some people already think Jews have. The goat's fur is thick and a little bristly, like the coat of a Jack Russell terrier. The fence confines his head on four sides, and I can't understand how he could have pushed it through. I tug at the wire, but the geometry doesn't yield. What was he looking for? Maybe a place without a fence.

According to the artist who is practicing letting go of anger, the phrase "to get your goat" derives from the practice of calming a skittish racehorse by placing a goat in its stall for company. Competitors wishing to spook the horse would steal the goat, thus "get your goat." The way to detach from anger, says the artist, is to recognize it as a moment and move on. On the road, I practice letting go of anger between encounters with cars.

The road is not well lit after dusk, so I carry a flashlight, and when I see headlights or hear tires whirring, I step off the road and wait. Sometimes a driver will lean out the window and say, "Be careful." People stop and say, "You shouldn't walk on the road at night." Their heads are bent at the angle they might use to speak to children or people with mental deficits. In Arizona, where I carry an umbrella in the sun, middle-aged men shout out, "It's not raining." I used to say, "You are welcome to my melanomas." Now I ask how their erections are going. Often they look affronted, and I say, "Yeah, well, nobody likes rude remarks coming at them from strangers."

I reach through the wires and position the goat's body closer to the fence. His feet are planted. His eyes are black, the lids melting. I love him and want him to love me in return. Maybe this is what goat love looks like. I work on the fence until there is a bit of room to maneuver.

In some traditions, the goat is a sexy satyr whose horns the devil has borrowed. In other traditions, he is sure-footed and represents escape from guilty feelings. I grasp one of the horns and ease it out of the cage. To release the other horn, I have to press the goat's neck hard against the bottom wire, and he does not squirm or bleat. I want my memory of the road to be about the goat, although the drivers are swimming in the love, and I have to pick them out like peas from fried rice. At last the goat is free. He looks at me for a moment, or maybe he does not. Maybe he has already kicked away the fence as he runs up the hill to join his mates. I sniff my hands, and they are sweet and sour, and I do not know if this is the smell of pleasure or pain.

DOG

The dog smelled and was ugly, a Yorkshire terrier with two snaggleteeth and a baleful under bite. It had a breathing disorder that caused it to make hacking sounds until it was picked up and slung over a shoulder like the pig in *Alice in Wonderland*. The owner of the dog was dying, and Rachel took it home. Rachel was lonely, and after a week she forgot the dog's smell and ugliness. If you said the dog smelled, she said she had bought special shampoo and you must be imagining it. She styled the dog's hair in a spiky variation of her own, and she carried it everywhere in a tote bag. In time her friend Paul said he could not listen to another word about the dog. He did not want the dog thrust at him when he visited or carted to his apartment when Rachel went there. Their relationship unraveled.

The dog outlasted other attachments. By the time it was fourteen, it was deaf and almost blind, and it had developed thick cataracts that made it look like a small, crazy-haired zombie dog. The hacking was continual. Still, Rachel was stricken at the thought of losing her companion, and I realized I would never understand her attraction to the most hapless and stricken creatures that came her way, although I might be counted among them. When two giant condominiums began construction on my block, my apartment became unlivable, and I moved in with her. At this point, the dog was listless and refusing food. In the course of a week, Rachel visited the vet three times, and again, frantic, she placed the Yorkie in the basket of her bike and pedaled from the West Village to Thirty-Fourth Street. When she returned, she did not see any responsiveness in the dog. She called out to me, and I went to the back room. Rachel said, "Look at Pepper. I'm afraid to." My friend was huddled against a closet door. Above her were two paintings she had done of solitary pigeons staring out. I thought of them as Rachel and me. I opened the blanket that smelled of the dog. It was indeed dead. Pepper's legs were stiff. Her tongue was hanging loose, and I had the hardest time not laughing.

RING

I discovered the jewelry shop on a small, winding street in Miltham, a mile or so up the road from the rehab hospital where Ann was installed. A series of strokes had reduced her to the condition of a large, angry doll. Members of Richard's family were clustered around her bed with its pulleys and wheels, and Ann was staring out sullenly or burbling something no one but Richard's brother could understand. I felt in the way.

I said to Richard, "I'm going for a walk." I had been with the family for five days. He shot me the look that says, I love you for who you are, but do you have to be her all the time? I walked down a road past grazing sheep that looked up with forbearing faces as I plucked a tuft of wool from a fence and inhaled the lanolin. The clouds hopped along. It was an English summer sky that can darken in a moment or suddenly brighten after a storm. In time I arrived at a market town with streets and shops and strangers to look at. There was a park, an old-fashioned bakery, boys and girls flirting outside a coffee shop. There was a jewelry shop with a long row of windows, each draped in black velvet like sets for a puppet show in which miniature people dreamed of taking lovers and out of nowhere stopped talking in the middle of breakfast.

Ann was sixty-one and weighed more than fourteen stone. Three months earlier she and Cam had been at home when she strung together a chain of mismatched words and could not walk. He called an ambulance. She was released from the hospital the next day. The following week she had a second stroke and was released again, only later that day to suffer a third, nearly fatal stroke. Cam was a social worker and was friendly with the hospital staff. He expressed no criticism of her care.

I liked Ann. I hardly knew her. She was kind, and I saw her kindness as a small rebellion against her husband, who took time trusting people. Once, at their house, as the brothers were bantering, Ann shot me a look, as if she wanted to ask a question or link arms. We were both outsiders of the Brooks clan. Ann was still an outsider in some ways after being married to Cam most of her life. She did not ask me anything. People said she was shy.

In the hospital, her eyes darted to Richard and me when we entered her room. Otherwise she did not move. She was in a wheelchair, wearing a blue cotton shirt and cropped tan pants with an elastic waistband that made them easy to pull on and off. Her sandals fastened with Velcro straps, and her toenails were clipped. The big toenails were thick and yellowed. Did she mind? Did toenails slip through the net of brain damage, or did they rattle around like loose screws? She could not swallow and every so often coughed up strings of saliva Cam dabbed with towels he kept stored in a plastic bag hooked on her chair.

He smiled and said, "Ann says hello. Ann is happy to see you, aren't you, Ann?" She grunted, her lips tight, as if she

My Life as an Animal

were working out a math problem. She could nod and point and sometimes thread together two or three words. Cam said, "Ann, do you remember Laurie?" She moved her head in my direction. Sunlight glinted off the railing of her bed.

When Richard and I were alone, I said, "Are you going to ask Cam what he thinks about Ann's care?" He said, "No. I'd be concerned he'd feel criticized." We were in Cam's back garden, where all you heard was birdsong. The house was at the end of a road that merged onto an open field, stretching to the horizon, and you felt on the edge of a desert or an emptied mind. Richard screwed up his forehead and said, "Even if Cam has doubts, he wouldn't want to live in your world. In America the rich get everything, and the poor get nothing. Here, it's Benthamite. Everyone is treated, and that sometimes means the care is not so good. People here believe in national health, including me." He leaned forward and smiled. "Of course with type 1 diabetes I'd be dead by now if I'd stayed."

Ann was fed through a tube. Even before the strokes, you would have cast her as the farmer's wife, mixing batter in a glazed bowl with a long wooden spoon. Cam said she could taste the liquid when she burped. Today's flavor was vanilla caramel. He leaned toward her, his body arcing over hers, and said, "You like that, don't you, Ann?" It was as if he were speaking for a dog and had cracked the code.

Richard's sister Nicky arrived with her husband and son. Nicky lived near enough to Cam and Ann so she could visit most days. Ann's leg began to vibrate, and Cam tried to quiet it with his hand. There was a low coffee table in front of Ann's chair. Cam looked around as if beginning a show and threw a ball onto the table. It bounced, and Ann darted out a hand and caught it. Cam said, "Well done, Ann." Nicky drew her hands to her chest and said, "Oh my, very good, Ann." She clapped softly. The moment was unlikely, not least because Ann did not move her body or react to having caught the ball. The catch seemed a reflex, a cat darting out a paw to swat a fly.

Next Cam set a board before Ann with wooden Scrabble letters and began composing a sentence, hoping she would respond with a message of her own. At the sight of the board, a red curtain moved down Ann's face and she burst into tears that plopped off her round cheeks down the front of her shirt. Cam wiped them with his hand, reaching with the other hand into a breast pocket for a handkerchief. Ann's unhappiness made her present. I thought if she was angry or hurt, she was in there somewhere. Even if she were, she would need attending like a newborn for the rest of her life. When Ann began to cry, I told Richard I was leaving.

I entered the jewelry store and looked in the cases. Jewelry speaks to you. It predicts the future you wish you had. There was a ring in my mind. It was always in my mind, the deco ring that had belonged to my mother, the ring that was stolen, the deco ring with a central diamond and four smaller diamonds on either side.

The store was near closing. It was a town where shops closed sharply at five, a small English town with an elegant jewelry store. I kept picturing Ann. She could point with her right index finger. As Cam wheeled her through the hospital, he cheered her for knowing the difference between left and right. He had taken to saying, "I have the words, but Ann has the memory," as if together they made a functioning mind, as if they were of one mind.

There was a photo album at the hospital. Several shots were of a tall, slender woman in a miniskirt with shapely legs and a wide-brimmed hat. The woman was not smiling as she rushed along, her long hair curtaining her face and falling past her shoulders. It was Ann on her wedding day, and she looked like a runaway bride, moving toward something or away from it. Cam had long hair and wore pointy, black boots. In one shot he was a few paces ahead of his bride-to-be, and he looked like a rocker in a local band with aspirations and a surly attitude that would consign them to obscurity. The image had the grainy feel of newsprint. The caption might have read, "They don't know the power of their beauty."

I spotted a ring in the fading light. Did I notice the diamond had a flaw, a crooked streak below the surface? Did the saleswoman point it out? She was slender and pretty in a chic, navy suit, a white streak waving back from her temple like a pennant. I slipped the ring on my finger, a gleaming, gold Edwardian ring with markings inside the band, a gold band with an old mine diamond in the center and two small sapphires on either side. I slipped it on and off a dozen times, turning it this way and that, looking at myself in a mirror. Whose ring is that? Who bought it for you? Could I snap out a paw and just take it?

I left the jewelry store and went to meet the others. On the phone Cam had said to come to the Enigma Café. I said, "Where is it?" He said, "No one knows." The Brooks siblings are famous for their puns. Driving along with Nicky one day, we passed a small private airport, and she said, "They're having trouble getting off the ground." The others were there when I arrived, and I took a seat between Richard and Cam. They asked where I had been, and I said I had walked around. The ring was in my bag in a box made of thick black board that fit inside my black heart.

Cam ordered a tea cake, crinkling his eyes at the waitress. She wore dangling silver earrings that peeked out of her sweep of dark hair. When she leaned forward to retrieve an empty cup, you could see her cleavage in the V of her vest. She was maybe a little old and world-weary for the job, but she had a rock-and-roll air, a little punk, a little like Ann on her wedding day. Cam nodded cheerfully when she delivered his snack, or maybe, now that he was on his own, it would suffice as his evening meal. He was missing a tooth. Would he replace it in his new life? The waitress set down a cappuccino that frothed high. Cam spooned up foam and licked the spoon, flirtatious with the waitress, playful with his brother's pseudowife, or girlfriend, or whatever I was, buttering his tea cake and whispering, "You can't have a bite." I wished Ann were here. Ann before the strokes, gazing out with her Buddha solidity. The enigma wife.

A man awakens as he has for sixty-four years, and he greets his wife with cool lips on a round cheek, and he regrets that her skin is not softer, and he sucks back the thought. They speak about the weather and groceries, and he sets her place at the table and deposits a soft bread roll on a plate and removes butter from the fridge, wishing she were slimmer, and he sucks back the thought as if he had spoken. After breakfast she gets ready to drive to the market. She is wearing trousers, a jumper, and a jacket, and she is downstairs and can't speak. He sees a window open and a bird fly out, and the bird is his life. The bird is his mind. Her mind is gone. She is never coming back. He feels set free, and he hates himself. He feels alone, and he misses his wife. He misses her round body and rough cheeks, and he makes a call to save her. He calls an ambulance, although he knows she is not coming back and he has nowhere else to go.

My Life as an Animal

At the hospital, Cam had pointed to a picture of Ann and said, "Marrying her was the best decision I ever made." At the café, he said he was looking forward to her return home. He had renovated the house for her wheelchair. They would sleep apart, and he would listen for her coughs through a baby monitor. Aides would help him wash and dress her in the morning and at night reverse the process. He had bought a new washing machine to keep up with laundry. Ann was doubly incontinent. On and on he went, eyes on fire. I wished someone would say, "Go ahead and cry, Cam, or shout your head off, or shut your eyes and sleep for a month." I did not say anything. It was not my place. No one could say for certain where Ann was. Cam said, "She's strong. She could live another four or five years," sounding like a scientist whose experiment had gotten away from him.

After leaving the café, we returned to Nicky's house, and I showed Richard the ring. We were staying with Nicky. We were on the bed. He said, "Why did you buy it?" I said, "It was an impulse." He said, "You never buy anything on impulse." I said, "I buy everything on impulse. It's just that I hardly buy anything because I'm cheap." He said, "What I am saying is, why did you wander off and buy yourself a big fat present when Ann may be dying?" I said, "I don't know." He said, "You left me." I said, "I know." I was not sorry. He said, "People here stay together as a family. That's what families do." I said, "Oy," taking his hand. The ring glittered in the lamplight. I said, "Maybe you are wondering what you are doing with someone who could buy an expensive ring in the middle of a medical crisis. I am the person who goes to the hospital gift shop while doctors are pulling the plug on her husband." He said, "Oy."

I held out the ring and said, "Do you think it's pretty?" He took off his glasses and squinted, turning my hand. He said, "There's a flaw in the diamond, look, a little crack." He scratched at it with his nail, and for a moment I thought he could damage it. I looked at the ring, and I could see the flaw, too, although the diamond still sparkled in its antique setting. I said, "But do you like the design? Do you think it was worth the money?" In the store, I had pretended the price was in dollars instead of pounds. I said, "Do you think I was taken?" He said, "I don't know it's worth." I said, "I keep thinking about my mother's ring." He said, "I wish you would let it go. It was just a ring." And then the bed slipped out from under me, and it was hard to catch my breath. I had a sensation of falling through space, and I wondered if that was how Ann was feeling all the time.

Once when we visited her in the hospital the brothers left her room, and I stayed with her. Her hands were by her sides, and I took one, and she pressed back a little. I rubbed a finger over her fingers in a secret way, and it reminded me of squeezing my mother's hand as a child, squeezing in little pulse beats as we crossed the street. I didn't love Ann. We were balloons whose strings had gotten tangled. She coughed and spat up saliva, and I could not find a towel in Cam's bag. I got some Kleenex from my backpack and wiped her face and neck. My fingers got wet. I let them dry in the air, wishing Ann had no need of me or anyone else, but there we were, travelers who meet on a train or in a hotel and strike up a conversation until the afternoon has become night.

THREE YEARS LATER ANN WAS NO BETTER AND NO WORSE. She was living at home with Cam, and his steadfastness, or holding pattern, or whatever you wanted to call it gave off a kind of light. If a person is there, it is clear. If you are with a vegetable, that is obvious, too. Ann occupied a third space. Her eyes followed you as she sat inert in her chair. How did you determine who was inside? Maybe she wasn't Ann, but she was someone.

Richard tried to like the ring, but each time I wore it he mentioned the flaw. I came to dislike it, too, and to enjoy disliking it with him. We were separated for a few weeks, and I was visiting friends in upstate New York when I entered another jewelry store. Behind a little Victorian desk sat a slender sylph with light-brown hair and the palest skin I had ever seen. I felt I could see through her and she could see through me, and I wanted the moment to freeze so I would learn nothing more that would change the feeling. I was wearing the ring. She took my hand and said, "That's lovely." I said, "The diamond is flawed."

She asked if she could look at it through her glass. I took it off, and she inspected it and said, "Old mine diamonds of this sort are rare. The setting is beautiful, and the gold and sapphires are very good." I asked if she could sell it for me. She said she could. I told her what I had paid, and she smiled and said, "I can get three times that amount." I liked that she knew about jewelry and that I did not have to know what she knew as long as I trusted her. I told her how I had come to buy the ring and how I had come to feel regret. She said, "The ring has had a life before you, and it will have another life after you. It will stay with me for a while, and then we will send it on its way."

And that is what happened, and the sylph and I became friends, and when I think of the ring I see her hazel eyes, and

I remember asking her how she decided to study gems and value old things, and instead of answering she said, "People come into my shop all the time and look in the cases, but you looked at me." I said, "You looked like someone who could break a spell."

WHEN
PEOPLE FALL,
I LAUGH

(after Édouard Levé)

At a certain stage of life I divided my belongings into "things I could not part with" and "things that were part of me." The first group included a granite table designed by a man I loved. The second group included my father's ashes. In the period before cell phones, I liked checking messages from pay phones. Their sweet-and-sour tang became associated with hope. Plot devices in narratives that rely on people being out of touch are no longer credible. In subways, I push back against the thighs of men who encroach on my space. On the street, if someone compliments me, I say, "Thank you." Growing up, I did not know what was expected of me by my parents. As I get older Marilyn Monroe appears more and more beautiful. When I meet someone, I feel I know them.

As I get to know them, the stranger they become, but by then I am used to them. I wear new clothes over and over until they are no longer new. A friend suggested I wear a different shade of lipstick. I did not want to think she was looking at my mouth. I asked Richard why some people are more interested in monkeys than other people, and he said, "Some people, when they look in the eyes of a monkey, see their relatives." When I was four, in a clothing store I picked out an expensive dress embroidered with strawberries. The saleswoman disapproved of a child so young making the choice. My mother remembered the incident because she told the woman to mind her own business. I remember the story because my mother stuck up for me. I like being a guest in other people's houses. When I offer my apartment to friends, it is because I have to. When a young woman quickly established she was teaching at a prestigious university and working on her third book, I disliked her. When she said her son was mentally disabled and her husband had recently lost a third of his body weight, I felt guilty. When she said, "I never wanted children," I thought we should be friends. In skiing, falling is flying. My mother used to say, "A leopard never changes its spots." I wondered why a leopard would want to be spotless. I hunted for the chocolate she hid behind books. Leopards don't have spots when they are born; spots develop for camouflage. On the coldest day of the year I said hello to a homeless man swaddled in a dirt-caked blanket in front of the Victoria's Secret on Broadway. He looked up under a mop of dark curls and said, "Another place, another time." I discovered I had been unfriended by a writer on Facebook when his name appeared among people I might like to know. There was his picture in a little box, with his dark eyes and a jaunty wool cap pulled low on his brow, as if where he lived it was permanent winter. When I met him I was in love and loved everyone. He didn't have a boyfriend, and I hadn't had one in a long time. When I realized he had unfriended me, it reminded me of times I had found myself alone on a set of swings, a stretch of beach, a park bench. When I was a child, puppets scared me. Puppets are closer in size to children than adults. By the time I was old enough to articulate this, I had grown interested in puppets as abstractions. Siblings can fall into a kind of love that does not change. It also cannot be used, like furniture in a museum you are not allowed to sit on. When I consider that most of humanity will drown in floods within the next forty years, I file this away with wild, apocalyptic predictions, even though the ice caps are melting and the likelihood of a deluge is great. I answered an ad on Craigslist for free tea and spices and arrived at a stately brownstone on Tenth Street. The man who had placed the ad said he was in the tea business and was giving away what he didn't need. He was small and recovering from a cold, and he sat at the end of a large table arrayed with teapots and books related to tea. I took a box of black tea mixed with lavender and a box of chai threaded with orange peel and spices. He offered me a new, enamel kettle I accepted for a friend. I was happy on the floor rummaging in his boxes. He said, "I hope you are dangerous," and I did not think I was dangerous enough, and I wondered if I would cross paths with a man who had broken my heart. He lived nearby, and I imagined he would encounter me with the loot and say, "This is the reason I had to let go of you." I say things I don't mean. I may mean them in the moment or tell myself I mean them in order not to appear a liar to myself. When, at fourteen, the psychoanalyst I was in treatment with took me into his bed, I wondered how he knew I would not tell my parents. I used to imagine I would die of cancer, but as I get closer to death I think less about how it will happen. I laugh when people fall, even if they hurt themselves, even if I am the one falling. I dreamed my father flew in through a window while my mother was out shopping. He said, "I can't wait," and we flew out together. Below us, Broadway swirled like a river. A friend said, "Can you imagine sleeping with the husband of a woman who was like a mother to you?" I said, "Yes, I can imagine doing that." I prefer eating on the street to eating at home. I consider the time it takes to shop, prepare a meal, serve it, eat it, and clean up a kind of death. I once ate three hash brownies by accident and went for a walk. When the air cracked open and I could not feel the pavement, I wondered if I was having a stroke. I used to visit the apartment of a friend and look at the leftovers in her refrigerator. They were moldy, but I was jealous of her going to the restaurants. After the man who made the granite table died, I had sex with a doctor two times and two times I cried. I have drawn blood in fights. When I used to look at my dog, I would see all other animals. I think shame is something animals feel, but animals do not feel guilt. I do not laugh at satire. I laugh at slapstick and farce. One day a man approached me in the Guggenheim Museum. He smiled and asked how I was. He looked like someone I might like to know with his warm, brown eyes and unbuttoned tweed coat, but since I did not know him I thought I had forgotten my life. As I walked down the ramp, I remembered the man's name and that we had worked together at the *Village Voice* and finally that we had had sex one night with an awkward aftermath. When I passed onto Fifth Avenue, I did not know whether I was relieved to have left or sorry I had missed the opportunity to pretend nothing had happened. Storm clouds over the desert are extra black, mak-

My Life as an Animal

ing up for the fact it seldom rains. One day Richard and I were running from lightning, and a white streak split my life in two. In my apartment, when I used to wait for the buzzer to ring, I would dance around to Jimmy Cliff singing, "the harder they come, the harder they fall." A friend had a cancerous lump removed from a breast. She was dark haired and pretty. As she unhooked her bra, she stood before me with her chin up. A divot of flesh was missing from her left breast, and I knew I would not forget the moment. She said she felt disfigured. I said she was beautiful. She did not have a boyfriend and neither did I. When my mother was in her nineties and close to death, she leaned against the door of her bedroom and said, "I wouldn't have had children if anyone had asked me, which they didn't." The remark makes me miss her much the way I missed her when she was alive. I think women who live in secular countries and conform to religious dress codes make the lives of all women less free and less safe. I love money as a possession as distinguished from the love of money as a means to the enjoyments and realities of life. John Maynard Keynes called this "a somewhat disgusting morbidity, one of those semi-criminal, semi-pathological propensities which one hands over with a shudder to the specialists in mental disease." I like the ragtag look of homemade signs at political demonstrations. I like the way alcohol makes you want to fuck away your life. I eat whipped cream even though I have high cholesterol. I don't think artificial intelligence will be any more intelligent than the other kind of intelligence. I fall asleep only if I have awakened early the morning before. I once rode the horse of a mounted policeman in Central Park. I think the act of looking is erotic. A friend said, "There are stories that are mine to tell and stories that are not mine to tell." I do not make this distinction. Richard said, "The problem with origin myths is they contain a story about the ending of things, too. People read into evolution a narrative that justifies human domination." I said, "My life will go dark if you die." He said, "No, it won't," and I could see what he meant.

CATCH

I passed a truck on Broadway filled with sport shoes. Next to the truck a woman was writing prizes on a wheel: "pen," "water bottle," "T-shirt," "shoes." She had shiny brown hair and looked fit. I said, "What is going on?" She said, "We are giving away free things." My heart leapt. My mother used to say, "Nothing is free. There is always a catch."

The woman at the wheel said she taught yoga. She looked calm, and it struck me that yoga doesn't care why you need to be calm. You could be calming yourself to commit a murder. I was wearing flip-flops, and the soles of my feet were black. I was on my morning walk with bed hair.

A crowd gathered around like birds on a telephone wire. The yoga teacher looked out and made a show of considering the group. Then she took my arm and said, "You spin first. You have waited patiently."

I had done no such thing. I had kept checking my watch and returning sharp little answers to her polite questions. Like I was going to work for a T-shirt or a pen!

The joggers and floaters wanted the shoes. People in wheelchairs wanted the shoes. The yoga teacher noticed that the rubber stopper was missing from the wheel and sent people to search for it. When it could not be found, she said to me, "Spin anyway." I said, "Whatever stops at the top can be the prize." She said, "Right." I gave the wheel a tug, and around it flew.

The wedge with "shoes" on it soared to the top and plunged to the bottom and up it went and down again. The wheel did not slow. As it was turning, the yoga teacher whispered, "I want you to win." I thought I had charmed her. Then I wondered if she took me for one of the entrepreneurial street people who had recently set up shop on Broadway. They camped on the sidewalk, wrote in notebooks, and pored over novels behind signs that asked for donations while they weathered "a rough patch." Every so often they looked up with bemusement at passersby in suits. My life wasn't all that different.

The yoga teacher was holding a shoe, and after the wheel had spun enough she stopped it with the shoe and called out, "You win!" It was as if the universe had rolled toward me, even though I don't believe in the universe. The yoga teacher said to a colleague, "Bring our winner a pair of shoes." I said, "Thank you." I was happy. A second young woman asked for my size and returned with a box. I slipped on silver shoes with hot-pink soles and iridescent, green stripes, shoes I would never wear. Team members took pictures of my feet. I wondered if people would see my dirty soles.

The shoes were springy. I walked around, smiling, and I remembered being ten and asked to appear in a film about the new library at school. There I was with my pigtails and eager face. My mother had been a shy, aloof person who did not want her emotions read. She was dead, and I wished I could show her the shoes. She would have said, "How did you win them?" I would have said, "Pity." She would have said, "That is the catch."

THREADS

One night when I was working for a small catering company we did a wedding on the Lower East Side in a venue that had once been a synagogue. The space was near Cannon Street, where both my parents, by coincidence, had lived as kids. According to my father, the street you grew up on shot you off like an arrow. There were socialist streets, gangster streets, and garmento streets. After the ninth grade my father left school to sell dresses on the road. Around this time, a cousin of his joined the Purple Gang.

If the street you grew up on shot you off like an arrow, where was I headed from sleepy Barnes Street, with its tidy lawns, birdsong, and salty air? I took to striding up and down the streets of Long Beach, feeling lonely and chased. Who knew why?

The Purple Gang were Jewish thugs who terrorized Detroit in the days of prohibition, first as vandals in their neighborhood, then as hijackers and bootleggers running booze down from Canada. During their peak years, they recruited hoodlums from Chicago, St. Louis, and New York (the cousin) and were responsible for some five hundred murders. They were brought down in the late 1920s when

Italian mobsters cooperated with the FBI and when one of their own testified against the leaders during a trial for a horrific massacre. Among the kingpins were the Bernstein brothers (Abe, Ray, and Izzy) as well as Harry Fleisher, Abe Axler, and Phil Keywell. Phil's brother Harry served thirty-four spotless years of a life sentence and was released in 1965 to find a wife, a job, and a rabbit hole out of history.

Jews became gangsters in America because they had been gangsters in Europe, famously depicted in Isaac Babel's stories about Benya Krik, the king of Jewish gangsters in the mythicized Odessa of Babel's youth. Jews became gangsters in the United States as a way to be American—ante up to other ethnic tribes and make a run for success. The gangster figure acquired noir appeal from the movies. Symbolically, he remains a tough little guy—a striver, a scrapper. He preys on the weak, but his crimes cannot be measured against the pogroms, concentration camps, and gulags authorized by governments. To a kid in the suburbs of the 1950s and 1960s, the image of a lawless, danger-courting Jew was sexy, as it was to Babel in cozy Odessa. My parents' generation had faced street taunts and discrimination as Jews, but for me, growing up amid well-off Jews, I did not feel risk in the category.

The floors of the former synagogue were splintery and creaky, the staircases steep and rickety. Plaster flaked off the walls. There were no banisters and not a single straight line. You had to concentrate not to bump your head sprinting between floors. But the place was beautiful, with a vaulting, domed ceiling and a romantic mezzanine that looked over a ballroom festooned with gauzy silk curtains and twinkling votive candles. It was easy to imagine weddings here in the days when my parents had run around as kids. It was cold that day, the gutters mounded with crusted snow, the air blue with ghosts playing handball against brick walls. Fine, dry snow swirled over frozen streets, holding its form like the fake snow in department store displays. I could see my grandparents bustling along, their hands chafed, winding through pushcarts selling hot chickpeas—*heise arbis*—and roasted chestnuts. The salted, greasy peas would be scooped into paper cones and secured at the bottom with a pert twist. The chestnuts would nestle in coals that cooked inside metal braziers, the shells becoming black as beetles, little tongues of flame dancing up and down like a violin bow over strings.

I saw my father as a boy, slapping a handball against a wall, impatient to pitch himself into the world. He plays with boys from the street of learners who will go to City College. Their sons will become professors and doctors, and their daughters will raise the children of such men and teach them to use the right fork for fish. They will employ cooks who can galantine a capon, layering the boned sack of flesh with nuts, fruit, spinach, and eggs—a color for each season of the year. They will hire staff to sweep up snow that doesn't melt. My father will don a double-breasted coat and a furred fedora with a wide brim and look like John Garfield (born Julius Garfinkel), a guy on the make who could play a gangster in the movies, a Jewish gangster, muscular and compact. My father will start his own business manufacturing coats for girls, and he will work out every day and smell of cologne as he smooths down the back of a coat, tugging smartly at the hem to make it fall right. Before customers know what has hit them, they will want to buy my father's coats, and he will collect the garments and place them tenderly in tissue paper, as if lowering a lover onto sheets. He will circle the box with twine and attach a handle to carry the parcel like a little suitcase, and he will shave the price, waving good-bye to customers and saying, "Wear it in good health."

At home I was not asked to make a bed, prepare a meal, wash a dish, or vacuum a carpet. My parents did not believe children were brought into the world to work.

The bride and groom were young and pleased with the event. It was a Jewish wedding, and there were pyramids of food prepared by chefs in white jackets. Asian and Mexican dishes, a raw bar, a caviar station, and an expanse of deli meat that seemed a block long. The guests floated around gracefully. There were no drunken uncles with toupees askew, groping teenage girls. No tipsy grandmothers in acid-yellow wigs, skittering around on high heels. Still, it wasn't exactly British high tea. From the synagogue's patina seeped the "beslobbered breasts" and "blobs of rampant, sweet-odored human flesh" Babel describes in an Odessa wedding.

I was fifty-four. I worked from three in the afternoon until one in the morning, up and down the steep stairs, balancing heavy platters for the buffets, crouching and dipping back to the basement. For the breakdown there was more walking, clearing, scraping, and hauling. I enjoyed it. There was something comforting about schlepping near where my grandparents had schlepped as sewers and pressers in the garment trade. After the party was finished I cleaned the kitchen, filling forty-gallon garbage bags and lugging them outside, wiping down yards of steel counters, sweeping tiled floors. After waiters took whatever leftovers they wanted, I dumped the rest. Hideous waste. For myself, I packed smoked salmon and several pounds of sliced corned beef and brisket, the kind of lean, dense delicatessen my mother used to buy on weekends. Stacked up in columns, it looked like money printed with the faces of my family.

My Life as an Animal

Two party planners stayed late with us, boxing ornaments and vases. They were responsible for transporting the presents and unused liquor uptown—all in all a considerable load. A van pulled up as our crew was hauling out garbage, and we helped the young women ferry boxes to the driver. The cartons overflowed onto the backseat, leaving only a small space for the planners and an empty seat beside the driver.

He wore a wool cap pulled low on his forehead. He had a lean, hawkish face with a thin nose and shrewd eyes, and he spoke in an accent I could not place. His van was tidy, and he was precise in organizing the cargo. I asked where he was going, and it turned out close to where I lived, north and west of the old synagogue. My shopping bags were heavy, and it would have taken a long time to travel by subway. The nearest station was blocks away, so I asked the driver for a ride, and he said, "Why not?" Jaunty. I don't know if he cleared it with the young women. I didn't thank them. They kept apart from us, the help, in the way people do, by relating to your body as if it were a surface to leave drinks on, by averting their eyes and barely whispering, "Thank you" for a large service.

The way I situate myself with working people and poor people used to drive my mother crazy. "You don't like yourself," she would say, and I did not contradict her, because, really, how could I? I would say, "You haven't been Queen Marie of Romania all that long. We come from peasants and schleppers." She would look surprised to have forgotten her life and softly correct, "Not peasants. They lived in cities."

It's instructive being the help, *instructive* being a word perhaps lofted by people who can slip in and out of the role, although anyone who labors in a uniform—even one that upgrades you on the food chain such as a doctor's lab coat—

knows the Pirandellian slippage into a set of assumptions and the pleasure of disguise when, inside, you feel yourself a volatile element, a pile of crispy leaves, a mutant replicant. Every minority person knows this feeling in a field of dominant others. What I mean by *instructive* is that working in a service job reminds you you are a wind-tossed snowflake with no purchase on permanence. When you contemplate mortality— even if you have an *easy* death at ninety-five in Marienbad instead of a brutal one at twenty in Auschwitz—everyone's story winds up haunted and ephemeral. What is the purpose of being reminded of this all the time? Nothing. There is no purpose, period, but let's not pull on that thread right now.

I was wearing a down parka over my tux jacket, and I looked clownish in the combination of finery and street, like a figure out of Vaudeville, like a character from a Beckett play. And I had these bags by my feet loaded with food and flowers. There was a bag lady aspect to me, definitely. The young women talked on their cell phones or murmured to one another behind the driver and me. I felt a connection to him, fellow schlepper, with his trim body and neat jacket—a garment, I could see, he hung in a closet rather than flung over a chair. Something wry and cagey leapt off him, a silky, familiar thing that licked my face. I asked if he owned the van. He said he did, and we began a conversation.

He lived in Queens. I knew that many Russians lived in Queens, and because I had recently traveled to Russia and wanted the driver to be Russian, I asked if he was Russian. He said he was born in Italy and had moved to Israel, where he lived until he was thirty. He said, "It is the story of the Jewish people, moving from country to country. We are Gypsies. We feel uneasy remaining in one place too long." He shot me a sideways glance. I said I was a Jew, too. For all I knew the

My Life as an Animal

girls in the back were Jews. To the driver, being a Jew was romantic, as if Jews moved from country to country out of wanderlust. He said he had moved to Israel to be among Jews and to the United States to be a stranger. I said I liked being where I didn't strictly speaking belong. We cruised up the FDR Drive. The water was shining under a winter moon, and lights from the bridges danced on little waves churned up by wind. I felt as if a force from the old neighborhood had reached out a hand and was saying, "You may be alone, but who cares, who cares, if you pick the right strangers?"

The young women wanted to be dropped off first. The driver explained their trip would be shorter if he took me to my apartment first. They sat with tight little mouths as I prepared a package of deli meat for the driver. He said he would have it for lunch the next day. We said good night, and he waited outside until I passed through the front door.

Upstairs I danced around, putting things away, not tired, not bedraggled. I told myself, Don't get all Blanche DuBois about the kindness of strangers. Don't fall in love with luck. It was just a lift between two snowy streets. But I wanted to connect the strands of the day that felt like they amounted to something: the Jewish wedding, the old synagogue, Cannon Street where my parents had roller-skated, the Lower East Side dealing out strivers, revolutionaries, and gangsters like cards in a deck, the van driver stamped with the boot of the Holocaust, as the lives of all Jews have been—all people on the planet, really, although not all as murderously.

At the wedding, a soft, padded sack had been passed around for people to deposit gifts in. Jews give money, a custom considered crass in some cultures. Money, before it is exchanged for something, is an advertisement for desire. Money is a symbol of freedom—the nothing a thing is before meaning is attached to it. The Jewish interest in structures of interpretation is owed in part to the long, Jewish experience of being interpreted by others, although this contemplation is hardly confined to Jews. I stashed the meat and salmon in the fridge, feeling Jewish—a sensation, at once tender and severe, that stuck to me like an oily smudge.

But almost as soon as the emotion stirred, I smelled something corny and nostalgic in it. I placed tulips, roses, and hydrangeas in the sink and snipped the stems. I gathered vases, and as I arranged the flowers I thought about the van driver. I had said I was a Jew so he would not have to translate himself. But I was establishing more. He was talking about history, and in history I stood with Jews because people hated Jews for being Jews. In this context, to say you were not Jewish would turn you into something else you were not, because there was no such thing as being a nothing, and besides I wasn't a nothing. Everywhere I went people saw me as a New York Jewish type. My syntax, the speed of my thoughts, the Yiddish I tossed around.

I didn't have a problem with that, but as an atheist I did not want people thinking I practiced religion or believed in God. When someone wished me a happy new year at Rosh Hashanah or said, "Happy Hanukkah" in December, I made them take it back with a speech about the kind of Jew I was and was not. I made them wish they had not tried to be nice. I did not think they were being nice. I thought they were trying to slot me somewhere so I would not be flying around slotless and upsetting the balance of the universe. Upsetting the balance of the universe was a job description I would have liked.

I set vases on tables, window ledges, my desk. I lit votive candles. The place looked ready for a lover, although no lover was coming. I cleared fallen petals from the sink and carried trash to the basement, feeling a second wind as I wondered how memory and personal choice could figure amid the seismic eruptions of history.

I sat on the couch. The living room ceiling rose up high above crown moldings. Flowers scented the air, their lines reflecting off the glass and granite furniture. Next to the couch was a pile of books, and on top was *On the Natural History of Destruction*, a collection of essays by W. G. Sebald. They were about coincidence and history, and I had been reading them before the party. I could see they were coloring my thoughts.

Sebald is interested in forgetfulness, and as a non-Jewish German he is trained on forgetfulness of the Holocaust. "I have kept asking myself what the invisible connections that determine our lives are and how the threads run," he writes.

What were "invisible threads," and how were they connected to forgetting? Did he mean the unconscious? Maybe he was saying, with a nod to Freud, that forgetting only seems random while, in fact, it is a structured activity. When we want to, we can misplace our torture and murder.

Snow was falling. A dog whined outside the Korean market. Otherwise it was still. Sebald writes about the contact points of small and large events, looking for a way to attach his life to history. As a German he is saying, I could have been one of the killers. Okay, I could see how he would, but passing him on the sidewalk of history, would a Jew have to say, I could have been one of the killed? Even in the realm of speculation, even in the realm of language, I did not want to.

He further speaks of "strange connections [that] cannot be explained by causal logic." Does he mean a planful universe? If so, this was worrisome, for the part of the mind that believes in a planful universe is just like the part of the mind that forgets. They are both activities of wishing for things to have a particular shape when they do not.

I went to the kitchen to make tea, and as water boiled I thought about the allure of metaphysics. It tempts you when, say, you wish to be rescued from a snowy street and a van pulls up. The refrigerator hummed, conveying a message without meaning. The elevator opened, and footsteps retreated down the hall: a narrative fragment without a story. A passage from Philip Roth's memoir *Patrimony* came to mind. His father is dying, and Roth takes a wrong turn and winds up at the cemetery where his grandfather is buried. It is where his father, too, will shortly be interred, and where he, in time, will join them. Roth is not sorry to have made the wrong turn. He writes, "I couldn't have explained what good it had done—it hadn't been a comfort or consolation; if anything it had only confirmed my sense of his doom—but I was still glad that I had wound up there. I wondered if my satisfaction didn't come down to the fact that the cemetery visit was *narratively* right: paradoxically, it had the feel of an event *not* entirely random and unpredictable and, in that way at least, offered a sort of strange relief from the impact of all that was frighteningly unforeseen."

Narratively right! What a great concept! The relief of patterns.

Another book was by the couch, *Savage Shorthand*, a study of Isaac Babel by Jerome Charyn that had been sent by the publisher. I opened it, and there, racing across the pages like a pack of yapping hounds, were all the threads of my day: tough Jews, unlucky Jews, the consequences of erasure, and the unprotected life. Babel was a Jew who had run with the killers!

On the advice of Maxim Gorky, Babel left Odessa to live illegally in St. Petersburg—before the Revolution, Jews were not allowed beyond the Pale. Babel assumed a Russian pseudonym and in 1920 traveled with the Russian cavalry as a war correspondent, riding with the Cossacks into Poland and the Ukraine. On paper, the Red Army was advancing the Revolution. In reality, it was slaughtering Poles and Jews. Babel had believed in the Revolution, which at first lifted restrictions on Jews. Riding with the Cossacks, he wrote in what Charyn calls a "savage shorthand," a pitching, violent present tense without direction or exit. He watched a soldier take the head of a Jewish man under his arm and slit his throat so efficiently no blood splattered on his clothes. He saw rapes, people begging and coldly denied.

Witnessing months of cruelty "crazied" Babel, in Charyn's phrase, and he crafted a Russian that aimed to destroy language, with its deceptive definitions and orderings—a language that viscerally dramatized the failure of words. For Babel, existence has no metaphysical purpose. Meaning arises from a shifting arrangement of relationships. With the Cossacks, Babel becomes a predator and feels the arousal of unbridled power. Even more transforming, he identifies with the Jews who are caged. He "haunts the shtetl," Charyn writes, "repelled by the poverty, the forlorn faces, the smell of excrement, yet drawn to these Ukrainian Jews, so unlike the round and jolly worshipers at the Brodsky Synagogue in Odessa."

Babel's identification with Jews at the bottom was the flip side of his bond with the defiant Jewish gangsters he would evoke in his Moldavanka stories—tales of mythically proportioned, cutthroat thugs who are wildly and humorously verbal. Living in the Moldavanka, a Jewish ghetto surrounded by czarist might, Babel sidles up to the guys with warlord clout. Riding with the Cossacks and coming upon shtetl Jews, he's presented with an identification riskier to his image of himself and to his survival. He says to these people, in effect, If you are in danger, then I am in danger, and if I join you in your risk, then we are both safer. Or at least together.

From this point on, Babel identified with gangster Jews and shtetl Jews, and their conversation inside him built an art of collages and clashing jump cuts—he later collaborated on screenplays with Sergei Eisenstein. In Babel's writing there is no connective tissue, no narrative arc, only a refusal to avert the gaze and the need to narratize. Is there a more evocative style to capture fragmented existence?

Milky light eased through the windows, and I could see the snow-laden branches of the tall oak outside. I read with sadness about Babel's arrest in 1939 on trumped-up charges of spying. His papers and unpublished works were destroyed, and eight months later he was shot by a firing squad. The full story of his murder wasn't uncovered until the early 1990s, after the fall of the Soviet Union and the release of KGB documents.

I closed the book. On the back is a photograph of Babel, taken in 1931 when he was thirty-six. He looks at the camera with a wry little smile, and his lips are sensual and full. The tip of his nose is oddly angled, like the nose of the Tin Woodman in *The Wizard of Oz*. Rimless round glasses perch on his nose and behind them glint warm, intelligent eyes looking for action. A wool worker's cap is pulled low on his forehead—like the cap of the van driver. What bread crumb trails do we follow, what songs, lilted in faraway mountains, do we hear?

For some people choosing an unprotected life could become a social action. You had to seize your opportunities.

In the kitchen of the former synagogue, the meat, sliced against the grain, looked like a lattice of small tiles, and it reminded me of the shingles of our house in Long Beach, and I remembered the sound of trash bins rolled over gravel, like low thunder that does not end. There I was with my plastic charms, and frozen ponds for skating in winter, and an army of gladiolas spiking up in July. There I was, unaware of my mother's life. I rose above the flagstone patio and swam over the house in the pattern of a figure eight. To the left the bay gently lapped the shore, to the right ocean waves came crashing. My mother was with me, and we had fish tails, and we were having a good conversation.

One day when my mother was cooking mushrooms in a skillet, they came to resemble my father's face and it filled her with joy.

I LIKE TALKING TO YOU, 2

For a few seasons, Richard and I watched a TV show called *Pushing Daisies*, a fairy tale about a pie maker with the power to resurrect the dead. When the pie maker touches a corpse, it returns to life for a minute. When he touches it again, it dies forever. The pie maker's power extends over animals and plants. If he allows something to live, something else nearby is sacrificed. He restores his childhood love, who has been murdered, but the two cannot touch or she will die for good. It is a story about desire that cannot be extinguished because it cannot be fulfilled.

To be brought back to life with a touch. The muscled arm of Michelangelo's God sweeping across the ceiling of the Sistine Chapel toward Adam's outstretched finger. Prince Charming awakening Sleeping Beauty with a kiss. The characters in *Pushing Daisies* do not question the magic or the nature of limits in fairy tales. You may have three wishes. You must prevail in three ordeals. You must answer a question with three parts, such as the riddle posed to Oedipus by the Sphinx. It is sweet, this life. Even riding in a tumbrel, we glimpse a red bird in a yellow tree.

One summer at an artist colony, I met a man who had written a book about sailing. He was aloof, a prima donna, and people teased him behind his back. On Medal Day— when visitors were invited to roam the studios—he banded with a group of us and after dinner proposed we go for an evening swim. No one took him up on it but me. On the drive to the lake, he said his father was dying. I said my father had died. It was August. At the lake, a layer of insects hovered over water that was the same temperature as the air. We swam through weeds into a clear space, floating on our backs as light drained into the trees. We were there to say we had come and return smelling of lake. That night I thought the man had taken a step toward the group, but the next day he retreated and several months later was killed in a car wreck at thirty-nine, a week before his book was published and several months before his father died. How much time do we get to change?

RICHARD AND I ARE TEACHING A WRITING WORKSHOP together, and he says to a student, "Have you noticed that in several of your stories, the narrator claims she wants a boyfriend but it turns out she is happier with a bird?" The student blushes and bats her eyelashes, and Richard suggests ways she can dramatize her divided feelings. At home, he says, "I feel superfluous in the classroom."

We are in a café, and I suggest we imitate "The Despair of Art Deco," an essay by Geoff Dyer. Richard says, "I don't write dialogue well." I say, "Sometimes you do." He says, "That proves my point." I say, "You come from people who do not express what they feel. Their feelings live between the lines."

I peel back the covers and look at him. He pulls me close. He smells clean. He takes a lot of showers and he is not much of a shedder.

He says, "You shouldn't do the same thing every day." Before going to my desk, I slip on black yoga pants and one of several camisoles. In Arizona I walk the same course around a man-made lake. As a kid, I used to eat lamb chops every night. It got so I did not want to look at another lamb chop. I got over it.

Richard says, "I don't think my humor comes across in my writing." He sips a latte and settles the cup. He says, "There are some people I never believed in. Mickey Rooney is one. He had a mean look about him. Jerry Lewis is another. I never found him funny. If Dean Martin had shot Jerry Lewis I would've said, 'Let him off.'" I say, "That's funny. You were just funny. Write it down."

I say to him, "Stand by the tree. I want to take a picture of you and the tree." He says, "Why?" I say, "It's our tree. Remember when it was a dying stick in a black pail?" He says, "Someone left it by the hedge." I say, "You knew I would bring it home." He says, "I told you that. I wanted you to think I was thinking about you all the time." I say, "It was a ploy." He says, "*Ploy* is too strong a word." I say, "I believed you. I believe everything." He says, "I was thinking about you all the time." I say, "I was thinking about you all the time." I say, "Do you remember when Palmy's first frond unfurled?" He says, "I didn't study it as carefully as you." I say, "It spiraled open in the shape of the universe." He says, "To be honest, I don't care much about vegetation, or animals for that matter. I am confused if a fish is an animal, although I have advanced degrees in fields attached to the sciences. I seldom eat fish, although I fancy a kipper for breakfast from time to time. It reminds me of my mother. I do not think I spent five minutes in childhood wondering if she was happy." I say, "The tree is the same age as our relationship. We found it right after we met." He says, "You created the conditions of a rain forest." I say, "We called it Palmy." He says, "I think of the tree as Palmy, but I do not think if the tree dies it means we will die." I say, "Okay, but I want to take a picture of the tree in a happy period of its life."

I SHOW RICHARD BLISTERS THAT HAVE FORMED ON several toes. He says, "Get proper shoes." I say, "Clogs are proper shoes." He says, "They can't be, can they?"

He sits on the edge of the tub as I trim his hair. He says, "I have to fill out a form saying who you are." I say, "The girlfriend." He says, "Something official." We are teaching a workshop in London later in the year. I say, "Why don't we imagine things will work out?" He gives me the look. One winter Richard's mother relocated his hamster to the toolshed and Harold froze to death. She said, "Hamsters die. That's what hamsters do." Sometimes we say the opposite of what is required.

My shoes are in New York, and the blisters have formed in Arizona. In New York I shop in the closets of my friends. In Arizona I shop at yard sales. Recently I read about couch hopping. The couch hopper sweeps into a new city and sleeps on the couch or bed of a local person. Couch hopping promotes camaraderie and trust. There is the risk of people boring one another, but taking risks boosts the immune system.

I drive to a yard sale and greet a middle-aged woman in her driveway. She says, "Good morning." I say, "Good morning."

We smile. I find a pair of black leather mules with wide, rounded toes and cushioned insoles. What are the odds? I mean, really, what are the odds? The shoes look new. They cost a hundred and fifty if they cost a dime. I slide my feet in and think about times we are intimate with strangers. One-night stands come to mind, also Greyhound buses, summer camp, and prison. Richard and I moved in together right after we met. It was like an arranged marriage.

I hold up the shoes and say, "How much?" She glances away. Maybe it is embarrassing to sell your shoes. Maybe I am supposed to be embarrassed to buy hers. She says, "A dollar," and I reach in my pocket for a bill.

Back home, Richard says, "These are perfect." I say, "The straps are loose." He says, "Take them to a shoemaker." I say, "I want you to fix them." He says, "Okay." I say, "How will you do it?" He gets a hammer and a nail from the laundry room. I say, "Where did you find the nail?" He says, "In the toolbox." I say, "How do you know how to do this?" He says, "It's obvious." He hits the nail through the straps, and afterward the shoes fit fine. I think about how the right hand helps the left hand, and I wonder if Richard got to bury Harold.

WE VISIT A HIKING TRAIL CALLED DREAMY DRAW, AND it is hazy and still. The trail's name derives from the mercury mined there in the nineteenth century, *dreamy* referring to the effects of mercury poisoning—the madness of hatters, who used mercury to mold felt. We move through mesquite shrubs until emerging onto a scene of blooming cacti, thorny ocotillo plants with licks of flame shooting from their tips, and brown rabbits whose long ears have adapted to keep them cool by circulating blood. As we walk, dust gives way to red soil, and everywhere are rocks burnished black with desert varnish: sunbaked bacteria, the oldest living things containing DNA. Mountains in the distance look like giants around a feast, their backbones jutting into the sky. I carry an umbrella. Richard wears an old straw hat. Here and there a paloverde tree casts a small pocket of shade.

We are walking single file when Richard points to a dot in the distance and says, "It's a dog." I cup my hands and say, "A dog." When we walk and a dog appears, even on a leash, Richard pushes me toward it. Sometimes the animal is tiny and fluffy, a little puffball, a caterpillar scurrying along. I say, "Are you afraid of that?" He says, "It will bite me. It will go for my ankles. It will take one look at me and want to tear me apart." When I first learned about Richard's fear of dogs, I thought, I cannot love someone who does not love dogs. Then I thought, Maybe he will change.

He once told a story meant to explain the fear. He was five and at the home of his uncle Freddie in Lancashire. The town where Freddie lived was still Victorian, a mill town, a factory town with brick chimneys belching soot and pea-soup fogs. Freddie had a small black dog named Bobby, and at tea one day, as everyone was talking, Bobby ran up and down the parlor and spun around, barking with excitement. He dove into the shuffle of feet around the table, and some-one must have stepped on him, and he let out a yelp and shot toward the stove. He ran into the open grate, where coals were heating a kettle, and hot ashes showered onto his back. Freddie was up in a flash and grabbed the dog's back legs and pulled him out of the fire, knocking off red embers and burning his hands. The dog was crying. The hairs on his back were singed, and ever after there were patches where the fur did not grow right. Everyone looked on in horror, and then Richard's mum said, sorrowfully but almost

My Life as an Animal

lightly, "He had a fit, as little dogs do," as if the dog were responsible, as if no one had stepped on him, and Richard became afraid of the dog. I said, "Instead of your mother." He said, "That makes sense, but, really, I don't know the source of the fear. It is bigger than me and I don't want to give it up." We were sitting on the couch. He looked at his hands and said, "I have my father's hands." He said, "I think if the fear dissolved, it would produce a clearness I couldn't see through."

RICHARD SAID, "LAST NIGHT I HAD AN INSIGHT. YOU are on the spectrum." He meant the OCD spectrum. We were on the phone. I was walking. It was one hundred and ten degrees out, and I was darting toward slabs of shade under trees and beside cement walls. The grass was green, owing to the grounds keepers, who were wearing T-shirts embossed with cowboy hats. Richard said, "I mean, think about it: the cleaning, the organization, the ability to spot a speck of dust on the floor or a coin on the sidewalk, the willingness to re-write and rewrite until you are satisfied with the words. I am going to be more understanding." I said, "Okay."

I thought about the times I had said to him, "You have a thinking disorder." Or, "There is a disconnect between your hand and your brain, so when you pick something up, you do not know when you let it go. Keys, glasses, a wallet, a pen, the things a person needs when leaving the house. Sometimes it's your bag, or your jacket, or your backpack. It could be a car, a house, or a person." Our spectrums were traveling in opposite directions, like adjacent escalators, one going up, the other going down.

Still, if I had been walking on my own, I would have thought, Wow, it's hot, with every step.

RICHARD SAYS, "I WANT TO BUY A THERMOMETER FOR the pool." I say, "Don't we have one?" He says, "The pool guy broke it by accident." We are in the kitchen. In the window is a pot of watercress I bought marked down seventy-five percent. Who does not enjoy watercress in a salad or a sandwich? Richard is wearing a white cotton shirt with embroidery around the buttonholes. The shirt was designed by Wilke-Rodriguez and is a remnant of his marriage. I think the shirt represents their romance. He says, "Do I look like a waiter in this shirt? Would someone flag me down?" I say, "You look like a pirate." He says, "Let's go to Home Depot." I say, "We might as well buy bulbs for the front yard." The bulbs in those fixtures are tiny, expensive, and burn out quickly.

When we get to Home Depot, Richard says, "What did we come here for?" I say, "I'm not sure. I mentioned the lights after you mentioned the thing you wanted." Richard says, "This is bad. This is the end. It was only a few minutes ago." I do not feel that bad because the thing we came for wasn't my thing. Still, between leaving the house, stopping at the mailbox, and driving five minutes, we have forgotten the purpose of the trip. I say, "Let's walk around and see if something jogs our memories." Richard says, "Okay." We find the little lights and continue wandering, knowing it is futile. Several people in orange aprons ask if they can help us, and we say we have forgotten what we came for. A man strides along beside us and asks how we are. We say we are fine, even though we are concerned about our cognitive impairments. The man says he has an opportunity for homeowners. I say, "We do not own a home. We are homeless." We feel better.

My Life as an Animal

IN A MAGAZINE INTERVIEW, W. G. SEBALD DESCRIBED A rat experiment meant to illustrate hope. A rat was placed in a cylinder of water. It swam around for a minute, realized it couldn't get out, and died of cardiac arrest. A second rat was placed in a similar cylinder, only this one had a ladder and climbed out. This rat was then placed in a cylinder without any means of escape, and it kept swimming until it died of exhaustion. Sebald said, "You're given something—a holiday to Tenerife or you meet a nice person—and so you carry on, even though it's quite hopeless." He chuckled enigmatically.

I read the bits about the rats to Richard. We were in a café. His eyes darkened and he said, "Even if you discover something about hope from these experiments, you have to ask yourself, 'What did the scientist get out of causing a ratty heart attack in the first animal and sending both rats to the choir eternal?' No one interested in hope would place a defenseless creature in a hopeless situation. To be interested in hope is to care about when it succeeds. If you are organizing its failure, you are interested in suffering."

I said, "Wow, that's really interesting." I tried to imagine an experiment in hope, and nothing came to mind. Richard was defending the white lab rat, a soft, intelligent creature it was easy to identify with. White lab rats are albino mutants of the vicious, larger brown rat, and I was reminded of Joseph Mitchell's famous essay "The Rats on the Waterfront," written in 1944, in which he portrays an animal nearly as successful as human beings at dominating the planet—and without human technology.

Mitchell's rat is a force with more venom than purpose for it, an animal whose overkill exudes a Rabelaisian dimension. Brown rats can destroy the contents of a market on a stupor-inducing tear. They can gnaw through steel, bore a hole in almost any material, and squirm through spaces half their size. Harbor rats can run up a pole wielded at them and attack a person's hands and face. They like to bite babies because babies smell of food.

Despite such savagery, when I am away from New York, I miss my street-rat existence. I remember waiting in the subway after catering jobs. It is two or three in the morning and the subway musicians have all quit, and there are just a few of us leaning over the platform to spot a distant headlight on a train too far away to hear. Down on the tracks rats are playing in muddy water, fattening on chicken bones and pizza crusts and having the time of their lives.

Scientists have established that rats won't press a lever for food if the activity is paired with shocking a neighboring rat they can see. You cannot say you are powerless in love. If you are powerless, you are in a different kind of relationship.

My Life as an Animal

KOLKATA

On the phone the woman said, "I live on Frank Lloyd Wright."
I said, "Between what and what?" She said, "Near One Hundredth Street." She had a clipped, Indian accent that fell
over me, warm and intelligent. Her name was Rupa. She was
moving and had a rug to sell for five dollars. I thought it was
from West Elm and I texted to say I was on my way. When I
was halfway there, she texted to say she lived in a condominium complex and gave me the number of her building and
the number of her apartment. I wondered if she had withheld
the information on purpose, since these places are impossible
to navigate or leave. It was four o'clock, the crest of the day's
fire, one hundred and fifteen in the shade, although there
was no shade. When I arrived at One Hundredth Street and
Frank Lloyd Wright, I did not know which way to turn. I
turned left and looked for the number of her complex. It was
far from the turn. When I arrived at her complex, I could not
find her building. I asked a maintenance worker in a golf cart.
He shrugged and said, "I just started working here." I called
Rupa, and she said, "Park at the rental office. My building is just behind it." I did what she said and walked in the
sun with an umbrella. I passed a pool. A woman was drying

herself. I asked if she knew where Rupa's building was. She said, "No." I returned to the rental office, thinking I should leave, even though I had come this far, and I was reminded of the United States in Vietnam and how hard it is sometimes to pull out. I called Rupa again. She said, "I will come and get you." She sounded like she was singing. I did not think my voice could ever be that pleasant. It took her a long time to arrive, and as I waited I felt rusty filings of irritation collect in a pile at my feet. I called Rupa again. She was on her way. A little while later I saw her, a small young woman with long black hair and dark-brown skin carrying a little girl with long dark hair. The child's arms were draped loosely around her mother's neck, and her cheek was resting drowsily on her mother's chest. They got in my car, and Rupa directed me to her building. It was far from the rental office. She said she was from Kolkata and was moving back to her country after four years. I wondered about her sense of direction, her sense of place, her sense of dislocation, and as I took in how small and young she was, I stopped caring about the heat and the time it was taking to buy the rug. The little girl was pretty and stared at me mildly with giant brown eyes, as if I were an aunt she had never met come for a brief visit. The apartment we entered was a fist of ugly rooms, cluttered and messy with packing. When I saw the rug, I realized it was from Ikea, not West Elm. I did not want it. It was gray with white lines on it, and the material was thin. I said I would take it and gave Rupa the money. She rolled it up, wishing me the best of days. We asked each other questions until no more came to mind. I wanted to keep hearing the music.

HALLMARK

In Scottsdale, I mail packages at the Hallmark shop that sells caramel candies in a goldfish bowl beside the front register. There are pens with rubber angels at the end and a postal counter with two stations, where women left at the roadside of life, women with belly fat and dangerous perms, weigh and stamp parcels and say hello when you approach and remark that the heat is roosting over the desert like a giant brooding hen, or the heat is thinning and crumbling like a splintery old floor, or the heat is pouring down like fire over a mountain. They mention the thriller they are reading or the memoir about raising children who cut themselves. They ask about your day, and you say it is better for seeing them.

Except the German. She has hair the color of a rag streaked with rust and tied to a leaking pipe. Her breathing is labored and rattles with annoyance at each inhale. Her name is Edith or Ethel or Ethanol, or Ethelbert the Fierce. When I approach her, she does not speak. If I say hello, she frowns and looks through me until I hand her my packages. At first I thought she spread unhappiness evenly, like peanut butter on an animal trap. Then I saw she greeted some people with a smile.

One day she was weighing a package for me when she suddenly left the scale and helped a man who had come to the counter beside hers. His package was large. She had to walk around to where he was standing in order to measure it. He asked questions. She chatted him up. I stood there for a while. Then I went up to her and said, "What are you doing?" She said, "You moved back from the counter." I said, "I moved back to let you do your job. You have always been rude to me. I don't know why. You need to finish mailing my package." She did not apologize but returned to her counter.

From then on we used sign language, minimal and Kabuki looking, and I would strangle the impulse to say thank you when she handed me my receipt. And so it went, month after month, until the other day when I watched her striking the keys of her computer, her index finger tap, tapping like a little mallet, and I felt the weight of our dislike like a dead bird around my neck. It felt like the heat of August, where passion burns into ash. I leaned forward and said, "No one does a better job than you." She stopped tapping and looked up. "What?" She screwed up her face, huffing. I repeated the remark, and her wrinkles arranged themselves into a smile, and she said, "Thank you," and after she was finished she wished me a good day and I wished the same to her, and when I returned home I said to Richard, "I was nice to the Nazi." He said, "Why?" I said, "I don't know."

CLIP

The woman at the yard sale is thin and has white hair, a tanned face, her chest a little concave, a worried smile set like a clock that has stopped. She is wearing a striped shirt and white Capri pants, and there is nothing at the sale I want among the clothes hanging from the top of the garage or the tables spread with mismatched saucers and rickety eyeglass cases. Behind the white-haired woman is a younger woman with olive skin making change for a customer buying children's clothes. I say to the olive-skinned woman, "Do you have any jewelry." She says to the white-haired woman, "Don't you have jewelry?" The white-haired woman parts the curtain of clothes and darts inside. She returns with a plastic box containing smaller boxes and plastic bags. She places the box on a table and says, "I forgot to put it out." I peer into the box and begin to sift through the loot. She says, "What are you looking for?" I say, "Things that are old." She says, "I may have some." Another woman approaches the box, and I say, "I would like to look first, and then it's all yours." She moves away. The rules of the game. Inside the box are hoop earrings, strings of beads, and large broaches made of bright-yellow metal and chunky stones. Not for me. I also find a pouch of rings stamped with maker's marks that are hard to read. I say to the white-haired woman, "I am going to my car to get a magnifying glass." I point to the bottom of the sloping driveway. When I return, she says, "You are a professional." I say, "Not really." I inspect a money clip containing a coin with an Indian head dated 1910. I think the coin may be gold. The back of the money clip says 14K, but before that are stamped the letters JM. I don't know what they mean. I gather up the things I have put aside, including a bracelet that is beautiful although not gold, and I hold the collection in one hand with my fingers loosely curling up and say, "I don't think there is any precious metal here. Would you take ten dollars for these?" She says, "Yes," although I worry she is a little hesitant. I worry I have worked her. I worry she has been worked her whole life, and I worry in terms of character she has gotten the better deal.

BUS

Richard said, "Get a cab." He said, "Get an Uber." When he said, "Get a cab," I said, "I'll call you later." I was sweating, and my hair was frizzled. It was four o'clock, and there was no shade along the eight-lane road banked with baking vegetation and fast food. I crossed to the other side to wait for a bus. A woman was on a bench in the sun without a hat, her shoulders turning the color of a rib roast. She smiled and said a bus was due to arrive, and there it was, rounding a corner. The driver was large and beautiful behind the wheel with red lips and thick dreadlocks secured at the base of her neck. The bus was cool. I said to the driver, "A waitress gave me wrong directions to my hotel." She said, "Of course, a waitress," sniffing. I was in Orange, California, and I had walked eight miles the wrong way. I had a phone. I had GPS. Never mind. The driver's name was Joanne. She said the ride was on her. Once when I was trimming an agave in our back yard, I was bitten by fire ants. I thought the ants would not bite me because I was helping the plant. Joanne was full of life's happiness. I stood close to her, and when the bus stopped we looked in each other's eyes. It made up for the ants. The smell of roses wafted in and disappeared so quickly it might have been an illusion. Only poor people ride buses here. Everyone was a little rickety from exposure to the heat. I was watching movies about women who trekked long distances in scorching conditions with inadequate preparation. Why women? I said to Joanne, "I will not forget you."

HAPPINESS

I sent my landlord a letter through certified mail, asking to sublet my apartment. After two weeks, the letter had not arrived. If I moved out, Gertrude Wexner could triple the rent. If she stalled, she was betting I would move out anyway.

Monday morning I went to the post office. The supervisor had said, "Call me Monday morning." I called Miss Giles and was placed on hold. For thirty minutes. I was on hold, calling the place I was standing in.

Jean-Luc Godard observed that waiting is a form of enchantment. The seconds tick along like pulse beats, but time also stops, and you gain a kind of immortality. Maybe we are always waiting. When I told Richard about being placed on hold for Miss Giles, he said, "I would never have believed her in the first place." He does not expect service from service workers. "In England," he says, "workers hate providing service and loathe you for expecting it. The English accept this and muddle through, even if they are seething inside." They are always seething inside, which is why I could not live in that country. Every five minutes I would be causing a scene.

During my first few years with Richard, my friend Adam lived in my apartment and paid the rent. I told Gertrude he was my fiancé. She had beamed a yellow glare through her black-framed glasses but had not interfered. Now Adam had moved in with a woman, and I needed to install another tenant—this time legit.

In the post office, I was standing in front of a window with bars, and the radiators knocked and kicked. Behind the bars, the postal workers looked like bears at a shooting gallery, gliding along mysteriously. The window reminded me of a cage I had seen containing a snowy owl. I was in Alaska, and the owl had been rescued from an oil spill, and it stared out with its surprised owl face. I had flown to Alaska to help animals caught in a human mess, but it turned out I could not do much besides identify with the animals. People were swarming over the state, caring for otters and birds. It was better than doing nothing, I thought, because, really, what else can you think in a situation like that? The snowy owl was recuperating in a raptor center paid for by Exxon. People profit from disasters. To profit from disaster, you have to believe in the inevitability of failure. You have to think, more or less, like the English.

While I waited for Miss Giles, I felt like the snowy owl, squeezed between forces beyond my control. Richard favored shipping my belongings to Arizona, sublet or not. We had hired movers. I had sold my bike, furniture, hundreds of books. But of all the things I had ever considered in my life, moving my things to a place I did not want to live in seemed the craziest, and I imagined passing my file cabinets and couch in a revolving door as I swept off in a different direction.

The snowy owl had stood in its cage without flapping around, and as I recalled its stoicism—or owlism—a recent meeting came to mind. I was walking down Columbus Avenue, circling my choices, when I slipped into a L'Occitane shop. One of the attendants offered to massage my hands, and my heart leapt, and I thought, These streets are where I belong. The woman was wearing a tailored green suit from another age, something you find in a vintage store. She had been hired to give massages to anyone who entered, and I felt the hidden hand of the city moving out to embrace me.

I asked her what her name was, and she said, "Vicky" as she squeezed lavender lotion onto my hand. She said lavender was calming, and I sensed she needed to be calm as much as I did. She had a soft smile and large eyes, and as she worked I saw she was sad. She said she had been unemployed for two years and had lost her sense of self. I, too, had lost my sense of self in the desert. I asked how she coped, and she said she prayed, and I asked how she prayed. I had not asked this question of anyone before, but I was curious about her, and I wanted to show an interest in something she cared about. She said, "I petition God, and I believe he hears me, even if he doesn't answer." She said, "It gives me peace to imagine him listening."

Hearing her story, I was reminded of Beckett's play *Happy Days*, where, in act one, Winnie is buried in earth up to her waist and in act two buried up to her neck. Still, each morning, she welcomes another happy day because her love, Willie, is nearby. In reality, Willie ignores her and occasionally grunts an irrelevant remark. But anyone who studies the play will find analogies to their life. For example, I am grateful for Richard when I imagine myself alone in New York. I see myself pushing a shopping cart. I once thought of buying a metal shopping cart from two Taiwanese students who were moving to Indiana for jobs. I bought their microwave oven and an Ikea gooseneck lamp for reading in bed. I considered ferrying the objects home in their shopping cart. It was on the wobbly side, but really I turned it down because I got an image of myself as a doleful, wiry person plodding along behind the trembling contraption.

In the post office, I saw a similarity between waiting and praying, in that in both situations you are dangling before an answer. I was in front of window fifteen. I had rested my phone on the marble counter, certain Miss Giles was never going to arrive, and I began to cry. I wasn't embarrassed. I wanted to be a symbol of what the post office can do to you. I wanted people to look at me, although they were sealed inside the fortress of solitude New Yorkers erect in the face of chaos. Every time I thought of not crying, I cried more. Maybe it was a performance. Sometimes you do not know if you are acting. For example, I wonder this about people who say they have met their perfect mate. They are Romeo and Juliet or Lucy and Desi. But I wonder if, on occasion, they, too, might like to be in two places at the same time. In the post office, even if I was acting, I did not care. I was a New York character in a leather coat and blue-framed glasses. I was my mother, and I missed her because she was never going to enter my apartment again and ask why I was not married and publishing more. I wondered if we longed only for things we had no chance of getting.

The woman behind window fifteen disappeared without looking up, and after a while a new woman stepped into the frame. Her name tag said Miss Tuttle. She had light-brown skin, a crown of braid extensions, and a space between her front teeth. She had on a rust-colored sweater and a blue scarf tied stylishly at her throat. After a moment or two she leaned forward and said, "Why are you crying?" I said, "My landlord is measuring me for a coffin."

Maybe I was exaggerating, although I believed Gertrude

Wexner would not be vexed to see me carried out in a box. Over the years, several people in the building had died, and I could not recall a kind word from her to the tenants. I told Miss Tuttle about the envelope, the delays, and Miss Giles. Miss Tuttle stood up a little taller and said, "Go to window three. I will meet you there and help you."

I flew to window three while Miss Tuttle strode to the end of the bank of windows and stepped out the door. She put her arms around me and said, "It's okay, I'm going to call the stationmaster." She tilted her chin and said, "You can't be crying about an envelope." I said, "I know, right?" She said, "Relax, baby." She was like a mother. Not my mother, but someone's mother. I thought an answer was on its way, although maybe, as in Zeno's paradox, on each trip the answer could travel only half the distance between its origin and me—and therefore never arrive.

Miss Tuttle called the stationmaster on a walkie-talkie and asked him to meet us at window three. As we waited, we hugged again, and I felt something open in my chest. The envelope was still in limbo, but I did not care, and I became interested in the fact that one minute you could be panting after something and the next it could be hazy, and I could see that a substitution had occurred. Miss Tuttle had replaced the envelope. We rocked together, and when we pulled back, I said, "Why are you being so kind?" She said, "Because I am exactly like you. I feel things deeply. I am an emotional person, and I can't hold back."

I thought this kind of experience could not happen in Arizona. In Arizona, everyone was nice all the time. After the housing market tanked and retail sales went bust, friendly service was all that was left of the economy. This scene could not have unfolded in Arizona because people didn't rub up against you all the time. They kept their distance, and there weren't that many of them. I thought that for every Miss Giles there was a Miss Tuttle, and for every Gertrude Wexner there was a Vicky. In England, for every resentful clerk there was probably a beautiful garden. But for there to *be* a Miss Tuttle, there also *needed to be* a Miss Giles. It was part of New York's ecology of irritation, part of the way it made you grateful not only for civility but also for the feeling of rescue from drowning. I recognized myself. I was the place that had made me.

I said to Miss Tuttle, "Do you think we are supposed to hold back our emotions?" She said, "Other people might like it if we did, but that is not who we are." I said, "You are changing the course of my day." I thought she was changing the course of my life, but that sounded too dramatic, even to me. After Vicky finished massaging my hands, she had said, "I will pray for you. There is something you need, and I will pray for that." And I had thought, This is your way of saying we have made a connection. I wanted to tell Miss Tuttle something like that, and I said, "I will remember your smile and the feeling of your arms." I didn't specify for how long.

The stationmaster, Mr. Creighton, arrived. He was tall and dignified with deep creases in his cheeks. He was wearing a brown suit and a striped tie. All the postal workers looked worn-out. Maybe it was the fluorescent lighting. I didn't want to think about how I looked, my face streaked with tears. Maybe I had become the shopping-cart lady even without the shopping cart. Mr. Creighton said he would search for my envelope, and after twenty minutes, he returned with it in hand and said I could carry it to Gertrude Wexner myself. I said it had to go through certified mail for legal reasons. He said it would arrive in the afternoon. I said, "Thank you," knowing by then Gertrude Wexner would be gone.

Indeed, when the letter arrived, she was out of her office, and the mail carrier said he would return the next day. Now I was a character in Beckett's more famous play, *Waiting for Godot*, and it was time to pick up Richard at the airport. He was flying in to help prepare for the movers, who were coming on Thursday for a final estimate. I had borrowed a friend's car, and on the drive to Newark, I hit traffic. It took an hour to inch five blocks south on Ninth Avenue toward the Lincoln Tunnel, and as I sat in the snarl, I thought about the dwindling days I had left to sign the lease. If I signed it and could not install a sublet tenant, I would be liable for two years' rent. So what, you say. It's only money. You could look at it as a bet you lost in a poker game. I wanted not to care about money. I wanted to spend every dime I had and die with an empty bank account, but how do you know when you will die, and what if your money runs out first?

I was listening to WQXR on the radio, my old classical station, and I was happy to hear the music, but the traffic was making me feel stupid for clinging to New York. I called Richard to say I would be late and to arrange a spot to rendezvous, but his phone was turned off. His phone had been losing power, and he switched it off most of the time these days, which defeated the purpose of a cell phone, especially at a time like this. I thought he should swap his phone for a new one, but to him the thought of a swap, involving disgruntled store clerks or, worse, a superior-sounding voice in customer service, made his throat seize up. I thought this was idiotic, but what can you do? His phone was off the whole time I was driving out to pick him up, and by the time I found him at the arrival zone, I wanted to rip his head off.

I had to honk to get his attention, and as he ducked into the car and threw his suitcase on the back seat, a cop tapped my window. I was so incensed I didn't hear the tap, and Richard had to tell me to lower my window. The cop bawled me out for honking, and I explained about Richard's phone and apologized. Apologizing calmed me right down.

This was not the reunion Richard and I had hoped for, and as we snailed back to the city in more traffic, we had to work, each in a separate cocoon of misery, to remember why we were together. We had softened by the time we reached Manhattan. It was dark as we progressed north to my neighborhood. I found a parking space that was good for the entire time of Richard's stay, and I was feeling proud of the way I could find parking spaces when Richard opened his door and stepped into a wad of gum. The gum infiltrated the tread of his sole, and he cried out. He said he could feel the city sucking him into its bowels. What he actually said as he fought to unglue his foot was, "I hate New York." He said, "I hate New York," but I heard, "You hate Arizona." Then we held hands, making our way to a baleful restaurant we had not yet tried.

In the morning, sitting on the floor amid file folders and silverware, I wondered why people owned so much stuff. Our house in Arizona was practically empty, and I liked it that way. The last few weeks, while weeding out belongings, I had wanted to feel light and free, but as I was sorting I felt sorrow building, piece by piece, in the way that sorrow is a museum of sorrows. A single joy is not a museum of other joys. Joy is spontaneous. Sorrow is historic. Richard needed milk for his coffee, and I went down to the Gourmet Garage, where I bought bagels and goat cheese as well.

I was in the lobby, waiting for the elevator, when Gertrude Wexner leaned over the balcony of her office and crooked a finger for me to come up. Her red hair was in a bouffant

My Life as an Animal

style, flaming skyward, and I felt afraid. I realized I had always been afraid of Gertrude, and I wanted, finally, to be rid of the apartment. It would be worth it never to see Gertrude again. I walked up the stairs to her office and sat across from her. On top of her desk were pictures of a white toy poodle and a blond little girl. The poodle had sat in her office for years before it died. The child was grown, and we didn't see her around anymore. I thought Gertrude must be lonely, and her real estate was what she had, a building filled with people who wished for one of the loose gargoyles on the roof to come crashing down on her head.

She had put on weight, and her skin looked like it could use a sanding, like the floors in her apartments. She said my sublet request had arrived, and she waved the letter in the air, and for a moment I thought I was getting somewhere. But Gertrude's mouth was turned down, and the furrows between her eyes were deep. She said, "I don't believe you need to live somewhere else for two years, and unless you can prove this with signed affidavits about where you will be housed and working, I will refuse your request. In addition, I will need to see the tax returns for the past three years of anyone you intend to sublet to, as well as proof of their employment. If I find out you have signed a lease elsewhere, I will evict you." I said, "Why are you doing this?" She said, "Because I can."

Upstairs I told Richard about my meeting with Gertrude, expecting him to say, "Let it go. You don't need the aggravation." He said, "Get a lawyer." His voice was iron, his brown eyes flashing. Everything in him that did not like to be pushed around had come uncorked. Maybe it was New York. Maybe it was love. Whatever the cause, in that moment I wanted us never to be apart. I said, "Okay." He said, "I'll pay." I said,

"It's my battle." He said, "It's our battle." I said, "It is?" He said, "You don't have to ask."

I consulted friends about lawyers, and everyone said, "Call Harvey Finklestein." Harvey Finklestein had written the book on rent stabilization. When I called Harvey, he said he charged three hundred and fifty dollars an hour for the first hour. He hoped I would not need more time. He asked me who the landlord was. I said Gertrude Wexner. He laughed.

The next day I rode the subway to Wall Street. Harvey Finklestein's office was neither fancy nor plain. People in the waiting room sat with worried faces. Everyone looked as if one giant shoe in their lives had dropped and they were sitting there, suspended, waiting for the sound of the other shoe. When it was my turn to face the lawyer, he spoke quickly and to the point, and I thought, This is how he gets to charge so much. He said, "Legally, Gertrude Wexner can vet any prospective subletter as if they are a new tenant." He looked at me with his owl eyes and said, "The only way to maintain a rent-stabilized apartment in New York is to sleep in it half the days of the year plus one. Landlords can discover where you fly and where you use your credit cards. They can mount cameras in hallways and in the lobby and prove the days you are not there." As I listened, the room tipped, and my plans pooled in a corner. The artist I had lined up for my apartment was unemployed. Harvey Finklestein reached across his desk and shook my hand. He checked his watch and said, "You have some time left on the meter. You can email short questions if you like."

Back home Richard was on the couch, reading. I sat across from him and scanned the ruin of my place. Adam was a good friend, but he had left the walls coated with barbecue sauce and soot. Doors were broken off hinges. Walls were bashed and marked, pots burned, linens left stained and threadbare. You might have thought he was a rock guitarist instead of a shrink. Quentin Crisp liked to say, "After the fourth day of dishes in the sink and dirty clothes on the floor, a place smells the same from then on. You just have to wash after the fish course." The quip is amusing but inaccurate. In New York, if you don't clean for one day, dark grains collect on surfaces and fuzzy balls accumulate from God knows where and dance around your ankles like tumbleweeds. What would it take to restore my apartment? Did I want to?

Richard speaks about the natural history of objects, migrating in and out of museums. Inside a museum, an object becomes detached from its former uses. If the object leaves a museum, it may be able to circulate in the world again, but that seldom happens. In this way, people and objects are not that different.

Light straggled through a grimy window and lit up Richard's hair. I needed my city in order to feel alive, but I did not want to be here without my love. I looked into Richard's eyes and said, "I can't move." The words just floated out. His eyes were kinder than I had ever noticed, and I remembered something else Godard had said: "A film is a girl and a gun." Maybe so, but a film is also a change of plans. Richard said, "Live in the apartment." He sounded sincere, but who knows what resentment was already brewing? He was saying what I wanted to hear, and I believed him. I said, "How will we make it work?" He said, "We just will. You will be here as much as you need to, and I will come when I can." I said, "You hate New York." He said, "Sometimes." I said, "Why?" He said, "It's big and beautiful and rushing, and it makes me feel I don't belong anywhere. But you belong here. It's your home."

Maybe it was, but New York also scared me, and when I thought about being here alone I had an image of being eaten by an anaconda, slowly but thoroughly, so it would seem I had never existed. Richard said, "You need to be happy." I thought, I am happy. This is what happiness feels like. What else are you going to believe in a moment like this?

He began to unpack a box. I said, "I'll get rid of most of this stuff." I liked the look of the apartment thinning out. The living room would be light and open as never before. It would look like the hotel room at the end of the universe. He said, "Sign the lease." I said, "Okay," and I took it from the refrigerator door where it was pinned with a magnet. I signed both copies and slid them into an envelope. I went downstairs and slipped the envelope through a slot in Gertrude Wexner's door.

Have you ever made a decision you were certain of? Like in the movies, chin up, eyes forward? I have never made a decision like that. But as the envelope swished to the floor, I felt its power dissolve. Gertrude Wexner was powerless, too, as long as I paid the rent. Maybe she had been the MacGuffin all along. The MacGuffin is what Alfred Hitchcock called the device that launched the plots in his films. In a movie about thieves, the MacGuffin might be a necklace. In a film about spies it could be the contents of a package. A MacGuffin is the inconsequentiality that is both indispensable and of no real importance. It interrupts the waiting. It prompts the move from point A to point B.

My Life as an Animal

ACKNOWLEDGMENTS

Parts of this book were published in different forms in the journals *Fence, Anderbo, Open City, St. Petersburg Review, Exquisite Corpse, Joyland, Four Way Review, Threepenny Review, Superstition Review, High Desert Journal, Montreal Review*, and *Stone Canoe*, as well as in the anthologies *The Face in the Mirror, In the Fullness of Time, Book Lovers, They're at It Again, Best of Open City*. I am grateful to the editors.

Warmest thanks for my kind and loving residencies at Yaddo, the Virginia Center for the Creative Arts, the Millay Colony, Djerassi, the Edward F. Albee Foundation, Ragdale, and the Kimmel Harding Nelson Center for the Arts. These institutions have made my life possible.

Thanks to the friends who have listened, read, and written with me, especially Esther Hyneman, Wendy Sibbison, Deborah Maine, Margo Jefferson, Gail Davis, Timothy Schirmer, Andrea Blair, Ellen Kaplowitz, Susan Daitch, Marianne Rossant, and Emily Upham.

Several years ago I met Mike Levine, the editor of this book, at a party thrown by the National Book Critics Circle. We were in New York in early summer, and I was wearing a dress that looked like a caterpillar cocoon. Friends I had been staying with in Massachusetts had said, "Buy it," and I had said, "Okay," because dressing-room pressure is unassailable.

I had had a few gin and tonics at the party. They were free, and I am a friendly, cheap drunk. Mike was talking with an editor I had worked with at the *Nation*. I floated over. Mike was wearing a name tag that included his job with the press. I said something about my writing. I was networking. I was sort of drunk and wearing the dress. Mike handed me his card. I said, "Who is a writer you like?" He said, "Julie Hecht." I said, "I love Julie Hecht." I thought, If this guy likes Julie Hecht, that is a good sign. That is a good reason to send him my work, and I did, and he said, "Send more," and I kept doing it. He would tell me which stories he thought were building a book, and after we had settled on the manuscript I asked him what it was about the stories he had chosen because he had passed on some. We were speaking on the phone, and he paused to think, and there was time for me to wonder what he would say. He said, "I feel as if you are speaking to me and we are having a conversation, only you don't hear my part." I thought, This is perfect. This is best thing I could hear.

I send tender appreciation to the entire brilliant and talented production staff at Northwestern University Press, with special thanks to Marianne Jankowski for her sexy and witty jacket design, JD Wilson for his ingenious and enthusiastic marketing plans, and Mike Ashby for his impeccable copy-editing.

I will not try to convey my gratitude toward Richard Toon, without whom this book would not exist. First, because there would be no "Richard" character. We met nine years ago at Yaddo and soon after began writing together. Each of us in a separate notebook but in the same place at the same time. Then we read the pieces aloud to each other, and my life changed. My writing changed. We are still at the practice.

We sit in a café wherever we are and write to a prompt. We write a scene or a little meditative essay. Richard says things in writing he could not otherwise express. When we hooked up, we were pretty much strangers, and we came to learn about each other's lives through the writes. They have formed this book.